He's Watching

MARY PETERSON

Copyright © 2020 Mary Peterson
All rights reserved
First Edition

PAGE PUBLISHING, INC.
Conneaut Lake, PA

First originally published by Page Publishing 2020

ISBN 978-1-64584-188-3 (pbk)
ISBN 978-1-64584-190-6 (digital)

Printed in the United States of America

For my BFF—someone called me bossy once.
For my favorite bartender at BWW—Done and done.

Enjoy the read!
Mary Peters

1

Sarah Wheeler hadn't been back to Paradise since her family had moved to Chico about seven years ago. She drove back to what used to be her hometown. Everything was destroyed by the "campfire" that went through on November 8, 2018. She couldn't believe it! Her childhood home was ash; everything had burned. The town will rebuild, she was told, but it would never be the same. It would never be her "home" again.

When they left Paradise, her mother was engaged. Her mom was remarried now and loving life with her new husband, Detective Brad Hastings, who had been the detective in charge of Sarah's kidnapping case when they lived in Paradise. They bought a nice house in Chico where Lynda continued to sell real estate and Brad worked at the police station.

Sarah had gone to college majoring in law enforcement because she wanted to become a detective hoping to work with families of kidnapped victims. It was her life's mission to help find the victims and put the perpetrators behind bars. She knew what to look for, she knew the questions to ask, she knew because she had lived the nightmare that came along with being taken against your will.

She hadn't dated much after that year when was fifteen. Her old boyfriend, Luke, had turned out to be a sneaky, conniving, lying bastard that had hurt her deeply. She decided at that time that she would be just fine on her own. She had a great apartment in a secured building on the second floor with a balcony overlooking a nice yard where they had activities set up in the summertime for community engagements. While she had attended a few of the picnics/cookouts, she was always alone when she got there and when she left. She never felt like she was missing out on anything not having a man in her life only because she didn't want all the problems that went along with being in a relationship. Her mom and Brad had a wonderful relationship, and she envied it sometimes, but she had vowed that her guard wouldn't be let down ever again. No one would hurt or take advantage of her like the Jackson family had done.

Since moving to Chico, she had rekindled her relationship with her father and visited at least every couple of months. Her stepmom, Naomi, was actually pretty cool, but Sarah had never given her much of a chance before. Now that she was visiting more, she found out that she had missed out on a lot by not being around when she was younger. Her dad didn't really approve of her being a cop, but he did support her, and she was thankful that she could count on him being there for her if she had a particularly bad day. She really was lucky to have such wonderful support from her family and knew if anything were to happen to her, she had people to lean on, and for that she was very grateful.

She had been working at the police station in Chico for about four years starting as a 911 operator while she went to school to become a police officer. Her captain, Captain Layton, was the officer that had worked on a case years ago when her mom, who was selling a house, found a mysterious car in the driveway, which in turn led to the discovery of a dead man in the basement of that house.

She was working very hard to make detective; her captain knew what happened to her when she was a kid, so he also knew that it was very important to her to make detective. When she did, she wanted to make sure that all her cases were solved. She was going to be the best damn cop she could be, and no one was going to stop her! She was determined to pass her next promotional exam to become a detective. Her exam was scheduled for July 11 at 8:00 a.m.; that gave her roughly two months to study. She was studying, reading, and talking to her stepdad about what might be on the test. He offered to quiz her, and she jumped at the chance. He had been a detective for over twenty years, so she was pretty sure he knew his stuff. They made plans for the next night to get together for a study session and dinner. Lynda was going to be at a showing, so it would be just the two of them.

2

Sarah got home from the station, dropped her keys in the dish on the table by the door, and went directly to the bathroom. She started the hot water, stripped, and got in the shower. She let the water beat on her tired shoulders and thought about the day's events. She was still a beat cop, and that meant driving or walking around looking for trouble. For the most part, the beat she had was pretty quiet. A drunk and disorderly once in a while, but nothing juicy, nothing to sink her teeth into, and that wasn't preparing her for becoming a detective. Today had been different though. She started at 6:00 a.m., and it was quiet until about 1:30 p.m. when all hell broke loose. She was driving around downtown, going past the city plaza, when she saw people running out to the street.

Wonder what's going on in there, she thought. She radioed dispatch to tell them where she was and what she had seen. She told them she was going to go check it out. She got out of the car, checking to make sure she had her baton, gun, pepper spray, and radio. People were still running out of the plaza when she stopped one of them and asked, "What's going on in there? Why is everyone running?"

"There's a guy in there with a gun. He's been threatening people as they walk by, he's crazy!"

"Do you know who he is?"

"No, never seen him before."

"Where is he?"

"He's in front of the band shell. Talking to himself and then shouting. I was watching for a little bit and then decided that I was going to get the hell out of there before he decided he didn't like the way someone was looking at him. Glad to see that the police were called."

"No one called us, I just noticed people running and thought I'd come and check it out."

"Be careful and good luck!"

"Yeah, thanks," she said as she looked around for the suspect. *Crack! Crack! Crack!*

Panicked people started screaming and running around.

She radioed dispatch that there was an active shooter and that she needed backup. They told her to sit tight and wait, but she knew she couldn't do that. She had to see if anyone had been injured. She crept up to the band shell to see if she could see him. People were running and trying to find shelter. She had only heard him fire three times but knew that he probably had more ammo than that, so she was cautious. She peeked around the corner and saw nothing. She went around to the other side of the band shell and saw a man with a gun by the outside column. She drew her weapon and backed up so he wouldn't see her. Where was that backup? Come on! She might have to handle this herself. She watched him, and he was yelling and waving the gun around. She tried to see if he was yelling or threatening anyone in particular, but he looked to be alone, and he looked crazed! It didn't appear that there was anyone on the ground injured, but she couldn't tell from her location. She waited for what seemed like an eternity when she finally heard sirens. The guy heard them too, and he stopped to listen. They were getting closer, so he took off. Sarah ran after him, shouting, "Police, freeze!"

He didn't stop. She continued after him, gun still drawn, and told him again, "Freeze! Freeze, or I'll shoot!"

He faltered, tripped, and fell, his gun going off. She hurried over to him with her gun trained on him and asked him, "Sir, are you shot?"

No answer. She reached down to roll him over, and he tried to grab her arm. She jerked back, and when she saw the gun in his hand, she froze. He had it trained on her, and she feared the worst. She noticed his hand trembling, and she reached for his gun. He let go of the gun, and she noticed that he was gut-shot. It looked to be a pretty bad belly wound, so she radioed dispatch to get an ambulance down there stat. The other officers had arrived and were surveying the crowd to see if anyone had been hurt when the gunman had fired. No one had been hurt except the guy who had the gun. She was applying pressure to the wound so he wouldn't bleed out.

"What's your name, sir?" she asked the gunman. He didn't reply. She asked him again, still no reply. She was going to try to find some sort of identification, but just then, the other officers walked up to them.

"What's the status, Wheeler? Are you hurt?"

"I'm fine. He, on the other hand, is not so fine. When I yelled, he tripped and fell, and his gun went off and shot him in the belly."

"Ambulance was behind us when we were pulling up, they should be here any second."

3

The ambulance guys showed up a few seconds later and took over for Sarah. She took statements from the people that remained in the plaza and found that he hadn't been targeting anyone, just that he had been angrily walking around, threatening people, and then had taken off when he heard the sirens. She went back to the station, wrote her report, and was informed by her captain that they would be having a sit-down about this tomorrow.

Great, she thought, *just what I need*. After her long, hot shower, she went to the kitchen, made a quick bite to eat, and went to bed.

The next morning, she met Captain Layton in his office at 8:00 a.m. sharp.

"Wheeler, tell me what happened yesterday."

"It's all in my report, sir."

"I know it's in the report. Tell me about it. What made you stop, what made you risk your life to go in there alone?"

"As the report says, sir, I saw people running from the plaza, and I thought it was odd, so I decided to check it out. I radioed dispatch to let them know where I was, what I saw, and I cautiously approached the band shell to see if I could see him. I heard shots and knew I had to do something."

"Even after dispatch told you to sit tight? What were you thinking?"

"I was thinking that this guy might have shot someone and I needed to go find out if someone was hurt. Besides, dispatch knew where I was, I had to go see if I could find him. Once I located him, I watched him as I scanned to see if there was anyone on the ground.

As soon as he heard sirens, he ran, and I knew if I let him go, we'd never know why he was there causing all this commotion. I hadn't exposed my location to him prior to giving chase, so I was in no danger until I started to chase him. I had to use my best judgment, and if there had been someone hurt in there, I had to at least see if I could help them or catch this guy."

"Well, Wheeler, that's not the way we do things, you wait for backup! I know you didn't get hurt and this guy was probably in his own little world, but you still need to follow procedures."

"So if someone had been in there bleeding to death, you'd like me to just let them die? I'm sorry, sir, I can't do that. It was my choice to go in there with no backup, and I'd do it again!" she exclaimed

"Ok, Wheeler, calm down. So what's this guy's name? Do you know anything about him?"

"No, Captain, I don't know anything about him. I'm going to the hospital to see if he can talk to me yet. I called yesterday, and they said that he was in surgery, and it was touch and go. They also told me he didn't have a wallet or ID on him at all, so they don't know much about him either."

"Look, Sarah, I know how much you want to be a detective, and I hope you pass your next exam, but you've got to do things by the book. It won't do you much good to make detective and then get killed because you were leading with your heart. You're a good cop—no, a great cop, and I don't want to see anything happen to you, understood?"

"Understood, Captain. Can I just ask one thing?"

"Go ahead."

"What would you have done? Or any of the other guys that work in this station? You hear shots, you use caution. You see people running, you find out why. I did what I thought was right, and I'm serious when I say I'd do it again. It would have been smarter to wait, they weren't too far out, but when he ran, I just knew that I had to stop him. I don't take this job lightly, and when I make detective, I'll be the best damn one you've ever seen."

"I have no doubt about that, Wheeler."

"Thank you for saying that I'm a great cop too, Captain. It means a lot that my hard work doesn't go unnoticed."

"Get out of here, Wheeler," Layton said with a smile. "Go find out who this guy is and what he was doing at the plaza yesterday. By the way, I should put you on desk duty after that stunt yesterday, but I won't because no one was hurt except the gunman, and he was shot with his own gun. Close the door behind you."

"Yes, sir, Cap'n! Thank you, sir!"

4

Sarah made her way out of the precinct where people congratulated her on a job well done. She smiled all the way to the hospital.

Once at the hospital, she inquired as to where the man with a self-inflicted gunshot wound was that had been brought in the day before and if he could have visitors.

"What do you need to see him about?" asked the nurse at the desk.

"I need to find out who he is and what made him do what he did yesterday."

"I suppose if he's awake, you could talk to him for a few moments. He is heavily sedated right now due to his injuries. He is in room 834, bed 2."

"Thank you," Sarah replied to the nurse. She followed the directions the nurse had given her, and when she got to his room, she was surprised to find him awake. She grabbed a chair and sat by his bed.

"Hello there. My name is Officer Wheeler, I have some questions about yesterday if you feel up to answering them?"

"Mm, maybe," he said groggily.

"First of all, what is your name?"

"Robert Stone."

"Where do you live?"

"Durham."

"What were you doing at the plaza yesterday?"

"I was fired from my job as a lawyer yesterday, and I was contemplating going back and killing my old boss."

"Where did you work?"

His eyes had grown heavy, and he had answered the last few questions with his eyes closed. He didn't answer her question, so she asked again, still no answer. *Dang it!* He fell asleep before he answered. *I'll have to try to find out where he worked so I can talk to his boss.* She quietly left his room but knew she would be back to talk with him again. She got back into her cruiser and went back to the station. Her captain was in his office, and the door was open, so she thought she'd go tell him what she found out. Once she talked to him and told him her plans, he said that it would be a good idea for her to stay off the street, at least today, to see if she could wrap this one up.

She started calling law offices to see if she could find out who he worked for and what had gotten him fired. On her sixth attempt, she reached someone who said that yes, he had worked there. Sarah perked up a little bit and said, "Is it ok if I come down there to talk to someone about him?"

"Um, let me check and see if Jerry will be here later on. Yes, if you could come and see him around one thirty, that should work."

"Ok, great, I'll see you then." Sarah went and told Layton what was going on. She went back to her desk grabbed her keys and decided to go on patrol for a little bit before her meeting. Thankfully, today was very uneventful, compared to yesterday anyway. She arrived at the law office at one twenty-five, checked in, and waited to be called for her appointment.

"Officer Wheeler, Mr. Barnes will see you now."

"Thank you," she said as she was led to his office.

"Mr. Barnes? I'm Officer Wheeler. I'd like to ask you a few questions about a former employee."

"Nice to meet you, Officer Wheeler. Please call me Jerry. How can I help you?"

"Robert Stone was shot yesterday. I went to visit him today to find out what happened, and he said that he was fired yesterday. Can you tell me why?"

"Oh my god! Bob was shot? Who shot him? How did it happen? Is he going to be all right?"

"He was at the plaza yesterday, yelling and waving a gun around. I had seen people running, went to the band shell to see if I could see what was going on, and then I heard three shots. I didn't see him at first, but when I moved to the other side of the band shell there he was, pacing and shouting. He heard the sirens from the other cruiser and took off running. I gave chase, yelling at him to stop, he tripped, fell down, and was accidentally shot in the stomach. I need to know why he was fired. That was all that he told me when I was at the hospital today."

"He was let go because he wasn't producing anymore. He hasn't taken any new clients for over six months. We can't afford to turn business away, every time I'd ask him to take a new client, he'd say sure and never contact them. He's been having some trouble at home, and I was cutting him some slack, but I just couldn't continue to pay him when he wasn't doing anything."

"What kind of trouble was he having at home? Divorce, trouble with his kids?"

"It's his wife, she's having an affair. When Bob found out about it, he went a little berserk. He started drinking heavily and became verbally abusive to the other staff in the office. I can't have that kind of thing here. I had to let him go, it just wasn't working."

"How long had he known about his wife's affair before he went 'berserk'?"

"I would say it was a couple of weeks, maybe a month. He wasn't himself right after he found out, but he continued to work, and then he stopped everything, except drinking. I kept him on as long as I could, but after the verbal abuse started, I let him go. The other people in the office were complaining about him, he'd walked in on some clients and scared them when he started yelling at the attorney they were talking to. He was driving away business."

"I understand. What else can you tell me about him? How were his kids handling the affair and his behavior?"

"Oh, he and Amy didn't have any children. I'm sure that was one of the reasons that she decided to have an affair, she didn't work, and he worked all the time. They spent hardly any time together, and she had wanted kids, but it never happened. He was tested and found out that he was impotent."

"It's obvious that he took this affair hard, but why would he want to kill you? He said that's why he was in the plaza, deciding if he was going to come back to kill you."

"Oh my, that is very dreadful news! I hope he still doesn't feel that way. Should I be worried, Officer?"

"I can only tell you what he said to me. He's going to be in the hospital for a little while as he recovers. If you are his friend, maybe you should go see him in the hospital, to try to patch things up, try to get him to see a shrink or something."

"Bob and I have known each other for over thirty years. I will go visit him, and I will try to smooth things over with him. Maybe I will rehire him if he promises to get some help. Anger management is top on my list, maybe a grief counselor too. I'm just so shocked that Amy is having an affair."

"Can I have his home address so I can follow up with his wife and see if she has more to add?"

"Yes, of course, you can get all of that information from my secretary."

Standing, Sarah said, "Thank you, Mr. Barnes, if I think of anything else, I'll get back in contact with you."

"Thank you, Officer Wheeler, I appreciate you coming by. If I can think of anything else, I'll call you." Sarah stopped at the front desk to get Bob's information and proceeded to his house.

5

She pulled up to the house, which was a beautiful ranch style with an attached two-car garage. She went up to the front door and rang the doorbell. No answer. She rang again and listened, no noises coming from the house. There was a newer Buick LaCrosse in the driveway, but that didn't mean anyone was home. She went over to the car and felt the hood; it was cold. She went to the front door again and tried the knob; it was unlocked. She armed herself and pushed open the door.

Standing in the doorway, she called, "Hello, police officer. Anyone home?" No answer. She stepped into the living room, "Police. Come out now!" Still no answer.

Maybe no one is here, she thought.

She went back to her squad and radioed dispatch to get the information on the vehicle in the driveway and also asked for backup. They told her the car belonged to Amy Stone, and she lived at the address where Sarah was. Backup was about ten minutes out, so Sarah thought she'd take a look around outside. She walked around the front of the house; nothing seemed to be amiss. She went to the backyard and found a woman lying facedown in a lawn chair in a bathing suit.

She said, "Excuse me, are you Amy Stone?"

There was no answer. She walked over to the woman and shook her; her hand fell off the chair and landed in the grass. Sarah felt her neck for a pulse, no pulse. She radioed dispatch again and told them to send the coroner out as she had just found Amy Stone dead in the backyard. She didn't move the body, and when the other officers arrived, they went through the house. Soon they were joined by the coroner and a couple of detectives. The detectives asked who found the body, and Sarah said, "I did."

They did an interview with her, and she told them everything, starting with what happened the day before, her interview with Robert Stone and Jerry Barnes, along with what happened when she arrived on the scene. They asked if the house had been searched.

"Yes, the other officers and I did a thorough search to see if there was anyone inside. No one was in there, and she was here when I got here."

They thanked her and said they'd take it from there.

Damn, she thought, *I really want to see this through. I'll talk to the Cap and see if he'll keep me in the loop.*

Once back at the station, she was heading to the captain's office to see if he would keep her up to date on what was going on with that case when she saw that he was talking to Brad. No big deal, she headed to his office. Layton saw her and held up a hand motioning for her to come in.

"What have you got for me, Wheeler?"

"I interviewed the suspect. His name is Robert Stone, he's married and recently found out that his wife is having an affair. He wasn't keeping up at work or taking on new clients, so he was fired yesterday. I went and spoke to his boss, he explained how things fell apart at work, so I headed over to Mr. Stone's house. When I arrived, I knocked, no answer, called dispatch for backup, decided to look around outside while I waited, and that's when I found Mrs. Stone in the backyard facedown in her lawn chair. The detectives arrived. I gave them my statement, and I headed back here."

"Nice work, Wheeler. Is that all?"

"Yes, I guess."

"You guess? What is it, Wheeler?"

"I just want to know how this one ends. Is it ok if I help with this one if they need it? I won't get in the way, I promise, and I won't help unless they need me to."

"All right, Wheeler, since you're bucking for detective, I'll let you help if they need it, but only if they ask you."

"Roger! Thanks, Cap!"

What a hectic few days, she thought. Good thing it was dinner at Brad's; she didn't have a thing to make.

She arrived at the house about six o'clock, let herself in, and was greeted with a hug and a beer. "How's it going, Sarah?" Brad asked.

"Fine. You heard about my day today, and I don't know if Layton filled you in on yesterday, but it's been a crazy few days! How about you? Working on anything exciting?"

"No, same old stuff. I didn't hear all the details about yesterday. do you feel like talking about it?"

She told him what happened, and when she finished, he said, "Boy, that's more exciting than what I'm working on, that's for sure."

"I really want to know how this all plays out. How did his wife die? Was she killed? Did he kill her and leave her out there like that yesterday?"

"Hopefully it won't take too long for them to wrap this up. It might depend on how long Bob is in the hospital and when he can be interviewed again."

"I just wish that I didn't have to drop it and move on to something else. I can't wait until I make detective so I can actually work a case from start to finish."

"You'll get your shot, sweetie, don't worry about that. Hope you're hungry, I ordered a Jamaican Me Crazy from Farm Star."

"Great, I love their pizza! I hope you're right about me getting my shot at being detective. I sleep, eat, and breathe police work, I just have to make detective on my first try! I want this so badly!"

"After we eat, we'll go through some things and see how you handle them. You'll be just fine. I know you'll make it. You've tried harder than anyone else in that squad room, you deserve it."

"Thanks, Brad. I really appreciate having you in my corner. It's nice to have support from your family."

They chatted about nothing important, and when the pizza arrived, they ate. Sarah finished off her second piece and said, "I'm stuffed! Thanks for dinner, Brad."

"Agreed and you're welcome, anytime!" said Brad.

Just then the door opened, and in walked her mom. "Mmmm, something smells amazing! Oh, hi, honey. How are you?" she asked Sarah after dropping her stuff on the floor by the door and giving Brad a kiss hello.

"Hi, Mom. I'm doing good, how are you?"

"Oh, just fine, dear."

"Hope you're hungry, we just finished, and it's still hot."

"I bet I could put away a piece or two. So tell me, what's been going on with you?"

Sarah recounted for her mother what had been happening the last few days. Her mom's eyes got big a few times, and a couple of times she made comments, but she listened with interest as Sarah told her everything.

"She'll make detective soon too," Brad stated.

"I hope you're right, Brad," Sarah said.

"I hope he is too, but at the same time I wish you wouldn't. I know I said I support you, and I do, I just have a hard time not worrying about you! I love you and don't want anything to happen to you."

"Aw, Mom, thanks for worrying, but I'm twenty-three, I can take care of myself. I really wish you wouldn't worry, I'll be fine."

"Famous last words," Lynda said.

They visited for about another hour, and Sarah said her goodbyes and headed home.

6

The next morning, she headed into work to get her assignment for the day and was told by the captain that there was an open spot in the next testing session, and he asked if she would like it.

"When is it?"

"Monday."

"What? That's only four days away! I don't know if I'm ready for it."

"Trust me, Wheeler, you're ready for it."

"If you think so, then yes, I'll take the spot."

"Ok, I'll arrange it and take you out of the other session."

"Thanks, Cap! You made my day."

Hardly able to contain herself, she texted her family the news. All of them responded with well-wishes.

I can't believe it, I might actually be a detective by next week, this is a dream come true, she thought. She would take the next couple of days and study like crazy. The weekend was a blur. She worked, studied, worked, studied. *I sure hope I pass this test*, she thought.

Monday morning, time to take her detective's test. She was so nervous. She didn't know if she could do it.

"Yes, dammit, I'm doing this, and I'm going to pass with flying colors!"

Sarah arrived at the testing facility fifteen minutes before the test was given. She found a spot to take her test and waited for it to start. The first part was a hundred-question multiple choice test with an oral exam to follow. She breezed through the first test and was practicing for the oral exam over lunch when Brad found her and asked her how it went.

"The first part was a breeze. Now for the oral exam. I have to say, I'm a bit nervous. I'm just glad the first part was easy."

"Oh, the first part wasn't easy, you studied, and that's why it was easy. As far as the oral goes, if you did well on the written, the oral will be no problem for you. I have all the confidence in the world in you! You'll do great."

"Thanks, Brad! It means a lot to have your support. Well, I better get in there." She gave him a quick hug and hurried to the room for her oral test.

The panel asked her questions and wrote down what she said after every answer. It was nerve-racking, and it seemed like it took forever. When she was done, she was so relieved. Now to wait for the results. She found Brad when she was finished, and he asked how it went.

"Good, I think. It seemed like I was in there forever though. How long does it normally take?"

"It depends on how many questions and how many people are in there with you."

"There were four people, but some of the questions didn't seem like they were general questions, it's like they were getting more in-depth than I thought they would."

"Really, like what kind of questions were they asking you?"

"Stuff like what I do in my spare time and if I carry a gun with me at all times. I answered them truthfully, but I still think it's odd that they want to know what I do outside of work. Are they looking for certain answers to those questions?"

"That does seem a little bit weird, but it's been awhile since I took the exam, maybe they're looking to see if an off-duty cop is reliable in a pinch. I don't know though. It should be fine, I wouldn't worry about it too much. How do you think you did?"

"Up until those questions, I think I did great. I do carry with me all the time, but I don't do much other than work, so I'm not sure what they were looking for. I guess I'll just have to wait and see."

"You sure will. Now you get out of here before they put you to work. Those tests are tiring."

"You can say that again. I'm just relieved it's over. I hope I know soon."

"Depends on how many people took it as to when you'll know."

"Well, I'm going home and take a nap, I need to recharge."

"Ok, see you later, and don't worry about it, I'm sure you did just fine."

Sarah went home and did just what she said she was going to: she took a hot shower and a nap.

7

She was awakened to pounding at her door. *What time is it? After eight o'clock?* Oh man, she slept for like four hours.

"I'm coming!" she yelled. She looked through the peephole and didn't see anyone there. "Is someone there?" she asked. No response. What the hell?

She didn't open the door because (a) she was a cop and knew better, (b) she'd already been hurt by people she knew, and (c) she didn't know anyone that would pound on her door and then not be there when she answered.

She grabbed her phone to check and see if she'd received any texts about someone coming to visit. Nothing. Strange. She grabbed her service revolver and carried it around her apartment with her as she looked in each room. No one in the house, but where did the person who was outside go, especially if they heard me yell that I was coming to the door. She decided to call Brad and see if he would take a drive-by. She talked to him, told him how strangely she had been awakened, and then said there was no one there when she went to the door. He said he's be over in ten minutes. While she waited, she turned on the TV and caught the rest of the evening news. About fifteen minutes later, there was a knock at the door.

She called out "Who is it?"

"Sarah, it's me, Brad."

"Ok." She went over to the door, unlocked it, and let him in.

"Are you ok?"

"Yeah, just weird that someone would pound so hard on the door that it woke me up, and when I said I'd be right there, there was no one here. I also didn't open the door to see if someone was there because of what happened before."

"It's a good thing too, someone might have been looking for an empty apartment to rob."

"Why pound on the door? If I didn't answer, why not try to get in?"

"I have no idea. Have you looked around the apartment?"

"Yes, I don't see anything out of place, and the deadbolt and chain were still on the door when I came down."

"Good. Do you want an officer to come by and monitor tonight? Maybe this person will come back and try to bother you again."

"No, I think I'll be fine. I just don't know who that could have been."

8

Well, well, Sarah, had to call your stepdaddy, huh? Are you scared to be alone? Who do you think you need protection from, besides me? I'd protect you and care for you better than anyone in the world, at first. When he had pounded on her door, he was hoping that she would have opened it, but she had called out that she'd be right there. Not wanting her to see him before she opened the door, he took off. He couldn't tell her how he felt about her right now. *But someday, dear Sarah, someday you will know.* He stayed where he was until Brad left. Not long afterward, he decided it was safe to leave. He started the car and drove away, no one ever knowing that he was there.

9

After Brad left, Sarah made a light dinner, sat on the sofa, and ate. She was half expecting someone to come back that night so she'd know who had been at her door before, but no one did. *Well, that's it, I have to get some sleep. I can't wait for a mystery person to come back. Maybe it was the wrong apartment.* All these things were clogging up her brain, so she decided to do some deep breathing to try to relax. She was heading back to take another hot shower when there was a pounding at the door. She jumped, turned around, went to the door as quietly as she could and looked out into the hall. It was black. What the hell? She looked again, and it was still black. Someone had their finger on the peephole. She retreated, grabbed her gun and phone, and went to the kitchen. There was more pounding on the door. She called 911 to tell them there was someone at her door and they had their finger over the peephole so she couldn't see them. She also told them she was a cop and to not use sirens as she wanted this person caught. She texted Brad next to tell him that there was someone at her door pounding again. He replied that he'd be right over but she texted, no, they're sending a patrol car over. She wanted to go to the door so badly, pull it open, and shove her gun in the person's face and ask them what the hell their problem was, but she wasn't foolish. If that person was armed and they wanted to hurt her, all they had to know was that she was on the other side of the door. Most doors weren't bulletproof. Hers wasn't, so she wasn't going to give them the opportunity to hurt her. More pounding. Whoever it was sure was persistent. Maybe she should say something—no, last time she did that, they took off. She'd just have to wait until someone else showed up. She felt like a prisoner. It was awful, knowing that she couldn't open the door for fear someone would hurt her. She tiptoed back to the door, looked out the peephole, and saw a person all dressed in black walking down the hall. No one was in front of her door, but maybe the person walking by had seen them or maybe that person *was* them. She retreated and waited. About a minute passed when there was a knock on her door. She went to see who it was, and it was Officers Stuart Lang and Jake Black from the Chico PD.

"Hey, Sarah, we didn't find anyone lurking around out here. Are you ok?"

"Hey, Stuart, Jake, how did you get in without buzzing me? Did you pass someone all in black when you were coming in? It might be the person that was just at my door, they went toward the front entrance of the building."

"What? That's how we got in, some dude was leaving. Oh shit, lock up, we'll be back!"

They took off in opposite directions, able to cover more ground being split up. Lang rushed down the front stairs but didn't see anyone. When he stepped out onto the sidewalk, he looked both ways and didn't see the guy again. He called Black on the radio but got no response.

Weird. What is he doing?

He went back the way his partner had when they split up. When he rounded the corner, he saw him lying on the sidewalk. He ran over to him and saw blood on the back of his head. He checked for a pulse and radioed for an ambulance. "Officer down." Thank God, the pulse was there, and it was a strong one. Stuart shook him, and he moaned.

What a relief, thought Stuart.

"What the hell happened?" Jake asked as he tried to sit up but was extremely dizzy, and when he touched the back of his head, he felt blood.

"Looks like our perp knocked you in the head. How do you feel?"

"Like shit!"

"Just lie still, I've radioed for an ambulance."

"I don't need a damn ambulance!"

"Yes, you do, now just shut up."

The ambulance came, checked out Jake's head, and told him that he needed stitches and had to be assessed for a concussion. They loaded him in the back and took him to the hospital. Stuart went back to Sarah's to tell her what happened. She was floored. *What in the hell is going on around here? Was someone trying to hurt me again, or do they have me mistaken for someone else?*

When Officer Lang left for the hospital to check on his partner, Sarah decided she'd check to see if it was ok with her mom and Brad if she could stay with them for a few days. She called her mom and explained what was happening, and her mom told her it was absolutely fine for her to stay with them for as long as she needed to. She thanked her mom, went upstairs, and packed a bag for a few days, at least until someone could figure out who the lunatic was that kept pounding on her door and leaving. She really didn't have time for this kind of thing; she was trying to get off of street duty and to become a detective. Thankfully she'd already taken her test, so this wouldn't take her mind off of it.

Once at her mom's house, she went to the guest room and made herself at home.

Her mom came up and said, "It's going to be nice having you around for a little while. I feel like we don't get to spend enough time together. You're always working or I'm at a showing. It will feel like old times, better times."

Sarah walked over to her mom gave her a big hug and said, "I agree! We don't spend as much time together as I would like either, but as soon as I make detective, maybe that will change. I know my hours aren't going to be that great, but maybe better than they are now."

"You get settled, sweetie, I'm glad you're here."

"I really appreciate you letting me come over until this thing gets figured out."

"I would never tell you that you couldn't come here. Where my home is, your home is, simple as that."

"Thanks, Mom. I love you, you know that?"

"Aw, honey, I love you too."

"I think I'm going to get some shut-eye. I've got to try to figure out what is going on at my apartment. I don't want to be afraid to live by myself."

"I know, dear. You'll figure it out, I have faith in you. Good night, Sarah."

"Night, Mom, and thanks again." Her mom smiled as she left her to get settled and go to sleep.

10

He went back to her apartment about 3:00 a.m. and pounded on her door. No answer. He kept pounding, but he didn't hear a peep from her apartment. *Did I scare her so bad that she left, or could she already be at work?* Normally she didn't leave this early. He'd left for a little while when the cops had shown up. He had hit the one cop in the back of the head because he was way too close to finding him since he hadn't had time to make it to his car when they arrived. He'd better not push his luck. She would probably never say anything before answering the door again.

I'll have to think of something else to do to make her wonder if the boogeyman is real. He went back out to his car, got in, and took off. There wasn't much traffic at this time of day, so he did some planning on his way back home.

11

Sarah awoke the next morning feeling refreshed and determined that she wasn't going to stay at her mom and Brad's any longer than she needed to. She needed to find out who was terrorizing her at her place. They might need to set up surveillance to catch the person, and she was fine with being bait. When she got to the precinct, she went in to talk to the captain about what was going on. She told him everything and that she would be fine with being the one they used to catch him.

"After all, I am a cop. You won't need to put someone else in my place, I can handle it."

"I'm sure you can, Wheeler, but I want to make sure that you are safe as well. Let me think about it for a little bit, and I'll let you know what I come up with, ok?"

"Sure, Cap, that's fine. I have a few ideas on what to do with the guy, but I don't want to go to jail."

"That's why I want to think about it and come up with a plan. Do you think you want to go back to your place tonight?"

"Yeah, I might as well. I was just a little upset last night, especially after he knocked Jake out. If he doesn't come back, then problem solved, but if he does, I need to figure out who in the hell is messing with me and what they want."

"Ok, I'll have a patrol car come by every hour tonight to keep a watch out. Maybe we'll get lucky and catch him in the act right away before anything else happens."

"Thanks, Captain, I appreciate it."

She left his office, grabbed her keys, and went on patrol. Driving around, she had lots of time to try to figure out who was behind this. It couldn't be Larry or Luke. Even with good behavior, Larry still had two years, and Luke had four. Julia and Stella would probably be out by now, but would either one of them have anything to do with this? She didn't think so but couldn't rule it out. Maybe some added security cameras at her door would need to be installed so she could try to identify who the person was. They sold cameras that could be put in anything now. She was going to have to look into that when she got home this evening. Work was uneventful that day, which suited her just fine. When she went back to the station, the captain called her into his office.

"Here's what I think we should do," he said to her. "Let's get you set up with some other sort of surveillance so that we can record who comes and goes from your building. We can put it anywhere we want in the building and have it feeding right to the station. I also might set you up with a roommate for a little bit too."

"Whoa, a roommate? Why? I'm a cop, I can take care of myself!"

"It wouldn't be for very long, just until we catch the guy."

"That could take weeks or months. Let's try the extra surveillance first. I want the feed to come to my apartment though, I might be able to recognize the person by something they do. When I was driving around today, I realized that Julia and Stella are out of jail, and it wouldn't surprise me if Stella is stalking me again, but that would be stupid, Luke and I are no longer together, and that's the only reason she was so crazy back in the day."

"That's good information for the patrol guys to have. I'll make sure and give them the description of both of those women. Ok, I think we have a plan. I'll send over one of our tech guys tonight so we can get you all set up."

"Ok, I'll go home and clear out a spot for equipment to get set up and wait for him to get there."

"Wheeler? Be careful. I like you being around here and would prefer not to have to train in another cop."

She blushed as she walked out of his office. He's never been that nice to her or that concerned about anything that she did.

She arrived back at her place about 6:30 p.m. Carefully she scanned the cars, sidewalks, and surroundings for anything or anyone suspicious. Feeling relatively safe, she went to her building and let herself in. She ran up to her apartment, let herself in, locked the door, and breathed a sigh of relief. She dropped her keys in the dish by the door and went to change clothes and clean out a spot for surveillance equipment. When she went into the bathroom, there was a Post-it stuck to the mirror, and it said, "Are you scared?"

Not touching the note, she unholstered her gun and decided to look around the apartment. She searched everywhere under things, in things, and around things but found nothing. That was the only thing that was different about her place—that note. She called Brad and told him what she had found.

"Get out of there right now, come over here, and I'll go to your place for tonight."

"No, Brad. I've checked the place out, and it's clean. One of the tech guys is coming out tonight to put up a couple surveillance cameras so that maybe I can see who this mystery person might be. Layton also said that he was going to have a squad come by every hour to keep an eye out. Julia and Stella are both out of jail, it might be one of them."

"I don't like the idea of you being there alone. Can I just come and take a look around? It will make your mom and I feel better. You're very special to us, Sarah, and we want you around for a very long time."

"Ok, you can come and look around. I didn't take the note off of the mirror either. Do you want me to call the station and have another detective come over and collect whatever evidence he might be able to find, or do you want to do it?"

"I'll do the investigation on this one. Do you know which tech they are sending?"

"No, Layton said he was going to take care of it."

"Ok, I'll be over in about twenty minutes. Don't unlock your door unless you know who it is, got it?"

"Yes, I got it." She hung up and waited for him or the tech to get there.

12

Well, well, well. She was going to have surveillance and hourly patrols, huh? Sounds like a great idea. Glad I know about it now so I can avoid it. I'll really have to come up with something great now. He was happy to know in advance what she was doing, and the little bugs he had planted were going to come in very handy. *Apparently I scared her more than she let on.* Maybe he'd lie low tonight and make some future plans for her. They were going to make it harder for him now that they were putting in surveillance and stepping up patrols. He was in his car sitting right outside her apartment building when a guy with a police jacket and large case walked by toward the building. Hoping it was the tech, he jumped out of his car and thumped him on the back of the head with the butt of his gun. He had to work fast before drawing too much attention. He dragged him back to his car, put him in the back seat, tied him up, and threw a blanket over him. Grabbing the man's case and jacket, he buzzed Sarah's apartment.

Just my luck, he thought, *a way in without causing any commotion. This is way too easy.*

"Who is it?"

"It's Morgan, the tech to put in your surveillance."

"Ok, come on up."

"Thanks."

When he knocked on her door, she asked him for his ID. Damn, he didn't have ID to show her. He dropped the case and took off down the stairs and out the front door. He shoved the guy out of his car onto the curb and fled. That was close. *How could I be so stupid to forget his ID? I was so close to getting inside her place and show her just what she means to me.* He didn't think he'd get that kind of chance again.

Sarah thought it was odd that the tech dropped his bag and ran. *Oh crap, it must have been my admirer. How in the world did he know to expect someone at my place? Who would have known besides me, Brad, Layton, and the tech? How would that creep know?* Just then the buzzer went off again. "Who is it?"

"It's Brad." She buzzed him in.

As soon as he got to her door, she threw it open and told him what just happened. He ran back down the stairs to see if he could see anyone running down the street. He figured the guy must have a car nearby, so he decided to go look in some of them to see if he would see him sitting it in, watching the building. As he was going past some cars, he saw a guy half in the street by the curb.

"Hey buddy, you ok?" Brad nudged him. "Hey, are you ok?"

Groggily the guy responded, "What happened?"

Brad helped him to his feet, and they moved onto the sidewalk.

"I'm not sure, who are you?"

"Name's Nathan Drake, I'm here to install some surveillance for a cop that lives in the building."

"What happened to you?"

"I was walking up to the apartment, and someone tried to crack my skull open."

"Do you know who you were supposed to go see?"

"The name is on the work order in my case. Hey, where's my case?"

"It must be the one that's upstairs on the floor. Do you have any ID?"

"Sure," he responded, pulling out his wallet. Brad looked it over and told Nathan to come with him.

"Looks like you might be the right guy."

"Hey, did you see my jacket? I had on my police jacket when I got here, and now it's gone."

"Nope didn't see that anywhere," Brad replied as they were buzzed in to go up to Sarah's apartment. Sarah was in the apartment waiting for them when Brad knocked on the door. "It's Brad."

She opened the door and ushered them in, then shut and locked it again behind them.

"You must be the tech?"

"Yeah, name's Nathan Drake. Wow, do I have a headache! Who the hell did this?"

"That's what we're trying to find out. With the surveillance cameras you're going to put in, it might actually help us," Brad responded.

Sarah got Nathan some aspirin and a glass of water and told him to take his time and if he wanted to do it tomorrow, that was fine too.

"No, I'll get it done tonight, just give me a couple of minutes to get the bats back where they belong."

"Whenever you want to start is fine," she assured him.

After a few minutes he asked her who knew he was coming.

"Captain Layton, Brad, you, and me, why?"

He motioned to Sarah to get him something to write with. She retrieved a pen and paper, and he wrote, "I'll sweep for bugs too."

She nodded her head in agreement, took the note, and showed it to Brad, who also nodded in agreement. Nathan swept the apartment and found three bugs. He took Sarah and Brad around the apartment to show them where they were—one was in her bedroom, one in the kitchen, and one in the living room. Sarah was a little unnerved that someone had not only broken into her apartment but that they had bugged it as well. She texted Brad and asked what they should do with them now that they knew they were there.

"We'll take them out," he texted back.

Brad called in the CSI team to dust for fingerprints throughout the apartment along with taking the bugs they had collected out of her apartment.

Nathan asked where she'd like the cameras.

"Wherever you think they will do the most good," she told him.

"I think one down by the front entrance for sure. I also think that one on your balcony, one at the back exit, and one by the fire escape. If he is trying to get in, these would be the best places, and if he's trying, then we will capture it on video. Lastly, I'd put one on your door right by the peephole."

"Won't someone notice all these cameras everywhere?"

"Not the way I do it. You have to make them look like it was part of the structure. Don't worry, equipment has come a long way in fifty years. It will only take me a couple of hours to get them put up and then another hour to get things set up in here. Do you have a spot that you would like the monitors?"

"Yes, I'd like them right over here." She showed him the spot she had cleaned out in the kitchen's alcove.

"Looks like a good spot. Plenty of room for them in here."

13

As he sat listening to them introduce themselves to the tech that he knocked out, he was making plans in his head on what he could do now. He was waiting for them to say more about where they were going to put things, but there was no more conversation. He saw a couple of people get buzzed in that had CSI jackets on. *Well shit, they must have found the bugs, that's why it's so quiet. This is not good news. I've been watching her for months, and this is not good news at all. How am I going to get her alone? How am I going to get to her at all now? She seems to have people that will come running when she calls, but there has to be a way. I'll find a way. She can't be kept away from me.*

14

Sarah felt a little better knowing they had found the bugs and that was how he knew about the tech coming over. She decided to talk to Brad about changing the locks and how she could make her apartment harder to break into. Nathan had just come back up from installing the one down by the front door, had overheard her, and said nonchalantly, "Get a dog."

"A dog?"

"Yes, he'll hear the thing barking and at least not try to break in. Keep your window shades down so he can't spy on you, and lastly change your locks to something a little bit more state-of-the-art. It should look like a fortress to him if he decides to show up here again, and that may just deter him."

"Those are some pretty good ideas," she said. "What kind of locks do you suggest?"

"Get a Kwikset Smart Key. You can change the key anytime you want to without a locksmith, and the only option to picking it is drilling it out. You would notice that as soon as you came home and wouldn't go in if you saw the lock drilled, you could keep right on walking. I would suggest too that you lock your monitors up when you aren't here. If he gets in again and the monitors are locked, he can't wait and watch for you."

"You're full of great ideas. Do you have any others?"

"Do you have a boyfriend?"

"I don't see what that has to do with anything."

"If you have a guy coming over regularly, he might stop bothering you."

"Well, I don't, so I'll have to try some of the other things you mentioned."

"You're single? Huh."

"What's that supposed to mean?"

"Nothing, just someone like you shouldn't be alone."

"Someone like me? Who exactly is 'someone like me'?"

"Hey, I didn't mean anything by it. You're a pretty girl, and it seems a shame that you don't have anyone to protect you."

"I'm a cop, I don't need anyone to protect me."

"Sorry. I didn't mean anything by it at all. Would you want to have dinner with me sometime?"

Well, that came out of the blue. "Uh, right now, I just don't have the time, and with all this going on, I wouldn't be very good company."

"Ok, thought I'd ask. It would get you out of this place so you're not a sitting duck. You can't spend all of your time watching for this guy, you'll drive yourself crazy."

"I won't watch them all the time, and I'm no wallflower. I've got a red belt in martial arts, I have no intention of just lying down and letting this guy get to me. I swore a long time ago that my victim days were over, and they are. I'm prepared to give this guy a beat down if he ever shows his face around me."

"Whoa, slow down, I just asked if you wanted to go out to dinner. I didn't ask you to marry me."

"I'm sorry. I have been a victim before, and I won't let someone do that to me again."

"I'm about done here. Let's go in, and I can show you how to use all the equipment."

He led her to the kitchen where he showed both Sarah and Brad how to get things started, how to freeze the images, how to move the camera angles, and other things they needed to know to help Sarah look out for her stalker. Brad said good night and left now that he knew Sarah would be safer.

"Thank you for everything, Nathan, and again, I'm sorry for snapping at you."

"Hey, no big deal. I'm glad that I could help you out and that you will be safer now. Do you want me to come back and install that door lock for you?"

"No, that's ok, I can do it."

"Wouldn't you feel safer with someone here while it's being changed in case he shows up? You can't be watching the monitors and installing the lock and since the door will be unlocked, it will be a bad situation if you are alone and he shows up."

"He already knows that I'm setting cameras up, he just doesn't know where. Do you think that he would really take the chance to be caught on camera?"

"I've helped out a lot of people who were being stalked. Granted, the stalker didn't know we were setting up surveillance, and they were caught sooner rather than after something happened, but there are crazy people out there that want what they want and will not take no for an answer unless they are stopped. It just seems like a shame for you to be afraid in your own place. I still think you should have dinner with me too. Maybe if he sees you leave with someone, he'll give up."

"Ever since I was kidnapped seven years ago, I don't have much to do with dating."

"You were kidnapped? Wow, that must have been awful."

"It was, but I survived it, twice. I know there are crazy people out there. I've already dealt with an entire family of crazies. It's getting late, and I have to get up early tomorrow morning. Thanks again for everything, Nathan," she said as she walked him to the door.

"You're welcome. If you change your mind about going out, you know where I work." He smiled and walked out the door, only stepping away from it when he heard the chain get put on. *She's a very interesting woman. I'd like to get to know her better*, he thought. *She might not let me though. Sounds like she had to deal with a lot of shit at a young age.*

When he got to the exit of the building, he turned around and waved in the camera at Sarah as he left. She couldn't help but smile when he did. He was cute, but no, she wasn't going to give in. She had enough on her plate; she didn't need to worry about some man coming in and upsetting everything. He had left his card on the counter by the monitors in case she wanted to call him or had questions. Maybe when this is all over, it wouldn't hurt for her to go out for dinner. She thought about it as she walked to the bathroom to take her shower. Brad had done his best to clean up after CSI, but there was fine black powder everywhere.

I'm not going to worry about it tonight, she thought, *I'm too tired.*

15

She took a hot shower and went to the kitchen to look at the monitors. She didn't see anyone that looked like they didn't belong, so she locked the screens and went to bed. She slept for what seemed like ten minutes when she heard a pounding on her door. *What the hell was all that racket?* She didn't turn on a light, crept to the kitchen, saw it was about 3:00 a.m., and unlocked the monitors. There was no one at her door.

What is going on?

She rewound it like Nathan had showed her and saw someone all dressed in black in front of her door. The face was covered in an all-black mask. She watched to see which way they went when they left, right out the front door. She switched to the front door monitor and rewound it to see when the person might have gotten in. There they were, in front of the list of names, buzzing anyone who would let them in. Unbelievable, someone actually buzzed them in at three in the morning. She'd have to find out how to zoom in to see who the idiot was that let them in. She'd need to talk to the building manager and let him know that someone was letting in people they didn't know and what was happening. This way he could tell the other tenants not to do that anymore. Since she had seen him leave out the front door, she guessed it was ok to go back to bed. Locking the monitors again, she got back in bed and slept until her alarm went off at seven o'clock.

I'll need to call Nathan today to see how to zoom in and how to do a few other things with these cameras. After getting to work, she went right to her captain's office and first thanked him for sending Nathan over and to tell him everything that had happened after she got home yesterday.

"That's it, Wheeler, I'm moving you into a safe house! I'm not going to risk this guy getting to you and hurting you."

"I'm changing the door lock today, I'm going to get in touch with Nathan again and see if he can show me more things that I can do with those cameras like find out who is letting the guy in the building at three in the morning."

"I don't care what you *want* to do. You're moving to a safe house!"

"No, Cap, I'm not. I will not let this guy, or whoever it is, have that kind of control over me I'm going to talk to Nathan about a security system too and see what other devices he can come up with."

"Dammit, Wheeler! Why can't you just listen to reason for once?"

"Look, Captain, I appreciate your concern, but I will not let this guy ruin my life. I'm doing everything that I can to be safe. If you feel like I need a safe house, then put someone in my apartment with me, just don't take me out of there. We have a better chance to catch him there than anywhere else."

"One more chance, and that's it. If he comes by again, I'll personally come over, pack your things, and move you myself."

"Ok, you have a deal." She turned and walked out of his office, took out her cell, and using the card he left for her, called Nathan.

"Hi, Nathan, it's Sarah Wheeler."

"Oh, hi, Sarah. Did you change your mind about dinner?"

"Um, no, but I need you to help me with something. I need to change my door lock immediately, he showed up again last night."

"What? This guy is ballsy!"

"Yeah, that's what I thought too. Can you meet me at my place in an hour?"

"Do you just want to go now? I'm sure your boss will let you leave to go take care of this now so you can try to protect yourself from some stalker dude."

"Yeah, if you're free now, let's go now. Do you have any of those locks, or do I need to pick one up?"

HE'S WATCHING

"I'll grab one on my way over."
"Great, I can't thank you enough!"
"See you soon."

16

She hung up, called her landlord, and explained what was happening and that someone was letting in people they didn't know. He said he'd be over as soon as he could to address the tenants of the building. When she arrived at her apartment, she decided to park the squad right in front so maybe whoever it was would think that she had called the cops, not that it was her car. She got out of the car, noticed a memo taped to the inside door of the apartment building about not letting in people you don't know, and thought, *Wow, that was fast. Now maybe he won't get someone to let him in, maybe he wouldn't even try.* She went up to her apartment, looked at the lock to see if she could tell if it was tampered with. She couldn't, so she let herself in. Nathan was sitting on her couch.

"What the, how the hell did you get in here?"

"I picked your lock. I was hoping I'd get here before you so I could show you just how easy it was. I'm glad you're changing it."

"It was that bad? I always felt so safe here. After knowing the tenants let in random people, I don't feel so safe anymore."

"You are safer with the chain on, but a pair of bolt cutters will take care of that chain. Now, let me get this put in and see what else we can do to make this more like Fort Knox."

She smiled, went to the kitchen, and turned the monitors on. "Would you like something to drink?" she called from the kitchen.

"Maybe in a minute, almost done here." He joined her in the kitchen and asked for a glass of water.

She gave him a bottle out of the fridge and said, "Is there a way to install some sort of alarm on my door that if someone touches it, a loud, screaming alarm goes off?"

"Well, there is an alarm that we can hang on the doorknob that will make an alarm go off if the knob is touched. They also make them for windows, and it would be a great thing for your patio door. I'm sorry, I didn't think of those things last night, I guess I wasn't thinking clearly."

"After you got your bell rung, it's no wonder. Is there a way to zoom in to see who would have let him in last night? I'm not sure why I'm calling this person a him, it might be a woman."

"Let's look at the video from last night and see if I can teach you a few more things about it."

They sat in front of the monitors and watched what happened the previous evening and into the morning. Nathan was amazed that this guy was so bold. He knew why she kept calling the person a him, because it looked like a him. Slight build but didn't seem to be womanly. No distinguishing features that would differentiate between the two either. He showed her how to zoom; they got the name of who let the guy in; and watched him walk up to her door, pound on it, and walk away like he didn't have a care in the world.

"Wow! He is either very bold, very dumb, or a little of both. I agree, it looks more like a man than a woman, and most of these cases are men, so we'll just stick with that. Ok, someone needs to tell the tenants to stop letting people in unless they know who it is. I want to get those hanging touch alarms for you, and maybe we could get you a recording of a mean-sounding dog that might scare him away at least once."

"You know, after watching this, it makes me madder and more determined to catch this jerk! I just wish there was something about him that I recognized, but I don't. The clothes are baggy enough so I don't know if it's a man or woman, the black mask covers his entire face, and there is no distinguishing walk. This is making me crazy. What else can you think of that will help keep me safe?"

"Besides moving, you mean?"

"Yes, besides moving. Bad enough the captain wants to put me in a safe house."

"Really? Might not be a bad idea."

"I told him I was going to get ahold of you and you were going to help me with my security. What about a security system in addition to the ones for the door and patio?"

"I really think that if all this doesn't stop him, nothing will."

"Well, let's get it all done and see what happens. I don't think he'll ever be able to get in here again unless he actually breaks the glass on my patio door. I could always look at getting bulletproof glass, it's nearly impossible to break. God, pretty quick I'm going to feel like a prisoner here. Safe but a prisoner. I do have some concern that if he can't get in to terrorize me, what is he going to do next? I really need to be prepared and on guard all the time until this lunatic is caught."

"Doesn't sound like much of a life to me."

"No, it doesn't, but I'm not going to let him win, I'm not moving, and I *will* catch him! Thank you for everything that you've done for me to assure me that I am as safe as I possibly can be. This shit just sucks."

"I have a great way for you to take your mind off of it, have dinner with me. I'll take you anywhere you want to go, you have to get out of here once in a while, or you'll go stir-crazy."

"I appreciate you asking, again. I'm just not sure that I want to bring someone into this mess while I try to figure out how to handle it."

"Um, I'm kinda already involved here. Didn't I just wire your place almost like Fort Knox?"

"Yes, you certainly did."

"Then have dinner with me, please? It might do you a world of good."

"It might get me killed too. Have you forgotten that I don't know who this stalking madman is? Whoever it is could be sitting across the street watching the apartment right now. How do I know that when I leave here, he doesn't follow me? I just don't feel right being with someone else who could get hurt. Maybe when this is all wrapped up, I'll consider it but not right now. I'm sorry, Nathan, I wouldn't feel right if something happened to you."

"Fine," he said dejectedly. "Why don't you call me when you think you might want to go out to dinner, and I'll see if I'm available."

"I'm sorry, I'm not trying to hurt your feelings. Look, you're a great guy, funny and caring, but I need to handle this on my own terms, and having to worry about someone else is not how this is going to play out."

"I get it, ok? I'll leave you alone, unless you need more help with the systems that I've installed."

"Nathan, thank you for everything," she said and leaned over and kissed him quickly on the cheek.

He looked at her, stood up, pulled her up from her chair, put his arms around her, and kissed her, right on the mouth. She was stunned at first; it happened so fast. She resisted at first, but the kiss took over, and she gave in. She put her arms around him and returned his kiss.

God, she thought, *it's been way to long for this, and it feels so good.* She pulled away gently, looked up at him, and smiled shyly.

"Ah, sorry. I don't normally do things like that," she stammered.

"Obviously you enjoyed it as much as I did. Please, Sarah, please go out with me? I don't like to sound desperate, but I really think you'd have a wonderful time, and it will take your mind off of things that are happening around here. There's something about you that makes me want to be around you, to hang out. If the date doesn't go well, I'd still like to remain friends, so really, you have nothing to lose."

"Thank you." She turned bright red. Was it the kiss? Was it the nice things he was saying? Was it that she wanted to be with someone again? Her head swimming, she finally said, "Ok fine, I'll go out with you, but we have to be on guard the whole night, so it might not be as much fun as you think, and if anything happens while we are out, I want it on the record books that I told you it might not be a good idea."

"You'll go out with me? You've just made my day." He kissed her again, this time gently and slowly.

She pulled away reluctantly and said, "You better go. If our mystery person is watching the place, they may be getting pissed that you've been in here so long, and I don't want anything to happen to you because you're doing a job for me."

"Ok, I'll leave, but I'd rather stay." He held his hands up when she started to protest. "I would be a gentleman and sleep on the couch, unless you had other plans for me," he said, winking and laughing.

Her mouth dropped open when he said that, but then she laughed with him all the way to the door where she said good night and he left.

17

What in the hell was taking that guy so long in there? What were they doing to her place now? I sure wish they hadn't found those bugs, I'd know just what was going on in there. Her blinds were always shut now, cameras catching him coming and going, notes on the doors telling tenants not to buzz people in. I think I scared her a little bit. Good, I want her to be scared! I want her to feel like she needs protection because she does. She has no idea what I have in store for her. It might be a little bit harder to get to her now, but I will, when she least expects it, I'll get her. Finally, the loser that's been in there forever is coming out. Maybe I should knock him out again, maybe he'll think twice before ever coming over to help her again. Nah, he's not worth it. I have my eyes on the prize.

Nathan jumped in his car, elated she'd said yes. As he was leaving, he saw a guy in a car parked across from the apartment building where Sarah lived. He was just sitting there, not doing anything, and the car was running. *He must be waiting for someone*, he thought as he drove off. Never thinking it might be the person that has been stalking Sarah, he drove home, smiling all the way.

18

Sarah got up the next morning feeling optimistic after everything that happened last night. Nathan was good-looking, probably in his late 20's early 30's maybe. He was kind, had a great smile, a nice body, and seemed to like her. She was looking forward to going out with him, actually. She had never "been" with a man, but that kiss stirred something deep within her that she hadn't experienced before. She was a little scared but also excited. She'd take it one step at a time and see what happened. *Something brighter to look forward to than this crazy person that won't leave me alone*, she decided.

Ready for work, she went down to her car, jumped in, and headed to the precinct. She thought someone was following her, so she turned down a few different streets, watching to see if the car turned with her. After about the third turn, the car was gone, and she felt better, thinking to herself, *He already knows where I live and work, he's got to know what I drive, and it would be really stupid to try something in the middle of the day.* She arrived at the precinct, went in, and talked to her captain about how things were going at her apartment and what they had done. He was happy that her place was a lot more secure, and then he told her, "I'm assigning a partner to you too for the time being, at least until we catch this guy. Please don't fight me on this. I need to know that you're safe while you're home and while you're on duty. This nut job might think you're an easy target if you're by yourself, but that's not going to be the case. Once this guy is caught, we'll talk about you going it alone again."

"Whatever you say, Captain. If you think it will deter him a little bit, I'm all for it. I like my life and would like to continue to live it, so tell me who I'll be partnered with."

"I'm going to assign Shane Andrews to work with you. He's been on the force for about three years, and he's a good cop. I think you two will get along just great. Let's go find him and tell him the good news."

"He might not think that way if he hasn't had a partner before."

"He'll be fine. Like I said, he's a good cop, he likes to help out, and this will be right up his alley."

"If you say so, you're the boss."

"What's gotten in to you? You usually aren't this agreeable."

"I decided that I can't do everything on my own, and if you're willing to help me stay alive, then I will take the help."

"I'm happy to see that you are taking this guy seriously. He could snap at any minute, and I'd hate for you to be around him when he goes wacko."

They walked over to Shane, and Layton introduced the two of them and explained a little of what had been going on.

"I'm glad to help in any way that I can," he said.

"Good, go in and get your assignment for today, and I will make sure that you two are paired up until this is over. Be safe out there."

"Thanks, Captain," they said in unison.

The two of them went out to her cruiser to get her things. Layton had decided that if the guy knew where she lived, he may also know what squad she drove, so they were going to assign that one to someone else for the time being and use Shane's.

After Sarah and Shane left, Captain Layton called one of the guys assigned to watch Sarah's apartment.

"Do you have any news for me, Marty?" Layton asked.

"No, not really. I've been keeping track of comings and goings, but so far, it seems like the same people come and go at the same time. I'm going to walk around and see what cars are here and get license plates to see if we can figure out who this guy is."

"Good idea, I'll call Thompson and see if he has anything from last night. Keep up the good work, and thanks."

"No problem, Captain."

Layton called Jim Thompson and asked him the same thing.

"I don't have much, but there was a guy that approached the apartment building late last night, and it looked like he was having a hard time getting in. I thought maybe he had forgotten his key and was trying to get someone to buzz him in, but he never went into the building. I thought it was odd, so I watched to see what he would do since he couldn't get in, and he jumped in his car and left. About a half hour later, he came back and was able to get into the building. There was another person that seemed to be hanging around for a while, walking back and forth in front of the place, but someone came out finally, and they left together. Other than those two things, I've got nothing yet."

"Ok, keep up the good work. Oh, and Marty is going to start taking down plate numbers so we can run them and find out who owns the vehicles and if they live there or not. I'd like you to start doing the same thing."

"Sure thing, Cap. Anything else?"

"No, that should do it for now," he said as he hung up the phone. *I sure hope we can figure out who is terrorizing Wheeler*, he thought.

19

Sarah and Shane left in his squad car after they got their assignment for the day. It was a different section of town than what she was used to working, and it was kind of nice to have a change of scenery.

"So, Sarah, what's been happening?"

"Oh boy, I don't even know where to start," she said. She proceeded to tell him everything that had been happening recently up until last night.

He whistled and said, "Wow, that's unnerving. Do you have any ideas who it might be?"

"I have ideas, but the people I would've thought it was are still in jail. I don't date, so I know it's not an ex. I hardly go anywhere except work, home, and to my parents' houses. I'm really at a loss as to who would want to do this and why. I mean, there was this girl from years ago who was rotten to me, but she served her jail time, and I've not heard from or about her since the trial."

"Have you checked to see if she is living around here somewhere? Maybe she hired someone to scare you?"

"I haven't checked on her but told Layton about her yesterday, and he was going to look into it I think. I guess it would be easy enough to check out. I could see her doing something like that, but her beef with me was about a boy in high school who, by the way, is still in jail. I broke up with him before the trial, and I've not heard anything from or about any of them in over seven years."

"I would suggest that you start with her. A woman scorned and all that jazz." He looked at her, smiled, and winked.

"I really don't think this would be her. It just doesn't seem like her style. Don't get me wrong, she's mean and cruel, but back then, she did everything herself, she never asked anyone to be nasty to me, I think she liked doing it." She shuddered at the thought of what Stella had done.

"You cold?"

"No, just remembering."

"Ah, I see. So what else can you tell me about yourself? Are you married, have kids, pets, or plants?"

"Plants?" she asked and laughed. "Not married, no kids or pets, but I do have a couple of plants. How about you? Same questions."

"I'm not married, no kids, pets, or plants. Boy, after saying that, I sound like a real loser. Can't even keep a plant alive."

"Not a loser, just not a green thumb. Do you have a girlfriend? Or boyfriend?"

"Boyfriend? No. Girlfriend, we actually just broke up. She wanted a ring. I didn't want to go that route. I thought I might be destined to be a bachelor, but I think I just need to find the right one."

"How long did you date?"

"A little over a year."

"How come you broke up?"

"She was a little bit too possessive. Always wanting to know where I was. I couldn't ever do anything with the guys, she was super jealous, and she just seemed a little unbalanced after a while."

"Wow, she sounds like that girl from my high school. Although to be fair, she was told things that weren't true, but she decided to be the crazy one and kidnap me and the guy I was dating and threaten to kill us both."

"Oh my god, are you serious? That is crazy. She's the one you don't think is behind this, right?"

"Yes, one and the same," she said and told him what happened years ago. "When they were all sentenced to jail, I was one of the happiest kids you would have ever met. Now I feel like I'm that scared kid all over again, wondering why someone is coming after me."

"Well, we'll just have to catch the guy so that you can feel safe again."

"I sure hope that happens sooner than later."

"How come you don't date?"

"Sorry, what?"

"You said earlier that you don't date, how come?"

"I have no desire to be let down and hurt like I was back then. Although it was an awful time, it helped me to become the person I am today. It's the reason I decided to become a cop. I want to help the victims of crimes, specifically kidnap victims, because I know what they are going through. I know how they feel, and I think I can help them and their families."

"Not all guys are bad."

"No, they aren't, but I'm going to put myself and my career ahead of anyone else right now."

The day flew by. They got to know each other some more, had a few traffic stops but nothing major, and returned to the precinct.

After they finished up their paperwork, Shane asked, "Sarah, do you need me to follow you home?"

"Why?"

"Because you're being terrorized, and you should have someone close by in case something happens."

"Thanks, Shane, but no. Layton has a cop stationed outside of my building all the time now. Sure wouldn't like that assignment, sitting there watching the same thing all day. It's nice to know there is someone out there watching out for me though."

"Well, if you're sure. I'll see you in the morning."

"See ya, Shane, and thanks again, it was nice of you to ask."

"No problem, have a good night."

Sarah headed out to her car, got in, and tried to start it. No dice. She tried it again, but the car wouldn't start.

20

"Damn!" she said aloud. *What's wrong with it now?* she wondered. She got out of the car and was going to go back inside to see if Brad was there to give her a lift home when she saw Nathan. She called out to him. He turned around and got the biggest smile on his face when he saw her.

"Hey, Sarah! How's it going?"

"Terrible, my car won't start."

"Want me to take a look at it?"

"Do you know how to fix everything?"

"Not everything, but I can still look at it."

"Ok, if you want to, that would be great."

They walked over to her car; she popped the hood, and they both looked at the engine.

"Why don't you jump in, turn the key, and we'll see what happens."

"Ok." She got in, turned the key, and it did nothing; it didn't even turn over this time. "Great, now it won't even turn over."

"What did it do last time you tried?"

"Not much, but it did turn over. Would you be able to give me a jump so I can at least get it home?"

"Sure, but you'll want to get it looked at as soon as you can."

"Oh, I will, but I don't want to leave it here."

"Be safer here not being able to start than at your place. Why don't I take you out to dinner tonight, and then I can drop you off at your house?"

"I don't think…"

"Stop, Sarah!" he said, cutting off her protests. "If this guy is watching your place and doesn't see your car, maybe he'll think you're still working and will come back later on. This way we can have dinner, and you won't have to worry about a thing."

"Except how I'm going to get my car?"

"Why don't you take some time for yourself tonight, and we'll worry about it in the morning?"

"I don't know if this is such a great idea."

"It's a fabulous idea, I know it is because it's mine!" He laughed at her expression, put his arm around her shoulder, and steered her toward his car.

He drove a brand-new Toyota Rav 4. She semireluctantly walked with him and admired his new car.

"I really like this. How long have you had it?"

"I bought it about a month ago. I like it too. It's roomy, comfy, and gets pretty good gas mileage."

He opened her door for her, went around the car, and got in. He looked at her when he was buckled in and asked if she was ready to go.

"I guess so," she said. "Can we stop at my place so I can change clothes? I'd really like to get out of this uniform."

"I think you look cute in it."

"Be that as it may, I don't want to try to relax in my uniform. It will only take me a few minutes to change, and then we can go, please?"

"Ok. I'm coming up with you because I'd like to look at some of the footage to see if our friend was back today or even last night."

"How about this, I run up change, we go eat, and then you can come up after and we can look at it together?"

"Ok, that sounds good," he said as he eased out into traffic. "But I'm still coming up with you just in case he got in somehow, end of discussion."

"Wow, you're kind of bossy, aren't you?"

"No, it's called leadership skills. Besides, if I was down here and something happened to you when you were up there changing clothes, I would never forgive myself."

"Ok, you make a valid point. We'll go up now, and then after dinner, you can come up and we will go through the footage from the last couple of days."

"Where are you taking me for dinner?" Sarah asked when they got back to the car.

"What do you feel like?"

"I'm in the mood for Italian, how about you?"

"That sounds great! Does Crush work for you?"

"Yes, I love Crush!"

"Then that's where we're going to go."

They chatted as they drove to the restaurant. When they arrived, he hopped out and opened her door.

"You are ever the gentleman, aren't you?"

"My parents raised me to be respectful and, yes, a gentleman."

They walked into the restaurant, which wasn't packed yet, and were shown to a table.

"It's been awhile since I was here," Sara said as they walked to their table.

"For me as well, but I'm really looking forward to it tonight."

"So am I," she stated as he pulled out her chair for her.

They got settled and started looking over the menu when the server walked up, dropped off some waters, and asked if they would like something besides water to drink.

"Hi, yes, please give us just a moment to look over the menu," Nathan asked.

"Certainly, my name is Tiffany, and I'll be your server this evening. I'll check back on you in just a moment."

"Thank you," they said in unison and laughed.

"So, Sarah, what are you in the mood for, wine, beer, cocktails?"

"I really don't drink much wine but would love a Mojito!"

"You know what, that sounds fantastic, I'll have one too," he said as he motioned for their server.

"Have you two decided what you'd like to drink?"

"Yes, we're both going to have a Mojito, and we'd like to start off with the fritto misto."

"Excellent choices, I'll bring out the Mojitos as soon as they are ready and order your appetizer for you." She left, and they continued to look over the menu, trying to decide what they'd like to eat.

"Everything, looks tasty, and I'm starving," said Sarah.

"I agree on both points. I think I'm going to have the chicken piccata. What would you like, Sarah?"

"I'm going for the bolognese. I haven't had it for a long time, and it just sounds amazing. Thank you for doing this and for what you've already done for me at my apartment. I really appreciate it."

"It's my job to make sure things get done right at your house. It's my pleasure to take you out to dinner. Here come our drinks."

Tiffany put down their drinks and asked about their dinner choices. They ordered, and as Tiffany was walking away, another server brought out their appetizer.

"That smells and looks fantastic," Sarah commented.

"It sure does. Here you go, enjoy!" Nathan said as he handed her a plate with some food on it.

"Mmmmm, this is delicious. Good choice!"

"It really is delicious. I've never had it before, but I'm really glad that I ordered it this time."

"So, Nathan, what made you decide to get into the tech business?"

"Well, I've always been kind of a geek when it comes to computers and things like that, so it was only natural for me to go to school for it and get paid to do something that I really enjoy. I took the job with the police department because it is very interesting and very exciting sometimes. I get to meet some pretty nice people, like you."

"Well, thank you for that." She blushed. "You're pretty nice yourself. I'm enjoying our evening, and oh, it looks like dinner is arriving."

Their entrees were put down in front of them, so they began to eat.

"Wow, this is outstanding!" Sarah exclaimed.

"Mine is pretty great too. Would you like to try it?"

"I'll try yours if you try mine."

"Deal," Nathan replied.

They put a little bit on an appetizer plate so they could sample each other's meals.

"Delicious!" they both remarked.

"So, Sarah, you were saying that you were enjoying our evening, and then what were you going to say?"

"Um, I don't remember. I lost all train of thought when I tasted my dinner, sorry."

They continued with mundane conversation while they ate. When they were done and the dishes had been cleared, Tiffany asked if they had saved room for dessert or if they wanted another cocktail.

Nathan looked at Sarah and asked her, "Dessert? Tiramisu?"

"Yes, please. It's my favorite!"

"Great, Tiffany, one tiramisu with two spoons."

As Tiffany walked away, Sarah asked, "What makes you think that I want to share?"

"You don't have to if you don't want to, I don't eat a lot of sweets, but if it's your favorite, I'd like to try it and see what it's like. I didn't want to order a whole piece because if I don't like it, then you will have to eat two."

"Oh, I see. I guess I can let you have a bite," she said and giggled.

"That's a great sound."

"What?"

"You, laughing, having fun, and not worried about anything."

"Well, you've done a wonderful job of making me forget my troubles if even for a couple of hours, which I greatly appreciate."

Dessert came, and they both took a bite.

"Heaven." Sarah melted a little bit into her chair.

"Well, that is very tasty. I bet I could eat an entire piece of this, but not tonight, I'm stuffed."

"You better not leave all this for me. You like it too, and it's only right that we share it."

"If you say so," he said as he scooped another piece off and laughed.

"Good idea you had for dessert, Nathan."

"Mmhm," he agreed with his mouth full.

They were finishing off their drinks and getting ready to leave when Tiffany brought over the bill. Nathan handed her a credit card, signed it when she brought it back, and tipped her generously.

As they were walking out of the restaurant, Sarah said, "Thank you for a wonderful evening, Nathan, I've thoroughly enjoyed myself and can honestly say that I haven't been this relaxed in days."

"You are certainly welcome. When we get back to your house, we'll look over footage from the last couple of days and see if there is anything on it that is worthwhile."

"Sounds like a plan."

They got in the car and drove the short distance to her house.

21

Once they arrived, they got out and went up to her apartment. She was unlocking the door when they heard her buzzer go off to let someone in the front door. She went in, pressed the button, and asked who it was. No one answered. Nathan ran down the stairs to the front door. There was no one there. He came back up to find Sarah at the monitors to see if she could see who had just buzzed her.

"Anything?" Nathan asked when he came back in.

"I'm not sure if I'm looking at it right, it doesn't look like anyone is there, but why would my buzzer go off?"

"Let's take a look and see." He clicked some keys, moved the mouse around, and brought the view from above the outside door up and zoomed in. "This is footage from ten minutes ago, let's watch this to see what happens."

They continued to watch the screen. They saw several people walk by, but no one stopped in front of the door. Just when they thought they had a mystery on their hands, a pole came into view and pushed her buzzer. There was someone attached to that pole, just out of sight of the camera.

"What the...?" Sarah asked.

"I don't know, but it looks like he knows or suspects that we have a camera set up out there." He froze the image, blew it up, and tried to see what kind of pole it was. It was grainy, but he was able to make out the bar code on it, and it looked like a paint roller extension. "Well, this might be something."

"What is it?" Sarah asked.

"Look, there's a bar code on that pole. We can call the detective in charge of your case to come and take a look at this and see if they can figure out where it was purchased or by whom."

"I'll call Brad, he's the detective and has been involved since the first day."

She took out her cell and called Brad. He answered sleepily, but as soon as he heard what Sarah had to say, he was wide awake saying he'd be right over and hung up. He let Lynda know what was going on and said he'd be back as soon as he could.

"I wish she would reconsider and come back and stay with us for a little bit, at least until you catch the guy."

"I do too, honey, but Sarah is a lot like you, she's stubborn and doesn't like to ask for help."

"I think that's a compliment, kind of? I'm proud that she is a strong woman. After everything that's happened to her though, I wish she'd be less likely to chase this person on her own and ask for help. Since she's asked you over, maybe she is realizing that she can't do everything."

"The only reason she asked me over is because the tech guy that installed everything was there when it happened, and he said to call whoever was in charge of her case."

"Oh? I wonder why he was there?"

"She said they went out to dinner."

"She's dating someone? She hasn't said anything about this to me before."

"Leave it alone, Lynda, she'll tell you when she's ready."

"I know you're right, but I'm still going to ask her."

"You go back to sleep, honey, I'll take care of things at Sarah's and be home as soon as I can."

"Ok, tell her if she wants to stay tonight, oh, never mind, I'll text her and tell her. Be careful, sweetheart!"

"Always!"

"Brad's on his way over. Thank you again for a nice time tonight, Nathan."

"You are welcome. Don't think that you're going to get rid of me that easily. He was probably here tonight, and I'm not leaving until

Brad says it's ok for me to go. Besides, I still have footage I want to look over."

"Ok, and for the record, I'm glad you aren't leaving just yet. I'm going to go change."

She went to her bedroom and changed her clothes. She put on a pair of yoga pants, T-shirt, and put her hair up in a pony. When she walked back into the kitchen, Nathan looked at her and thought for the hundredth time how beautiful she was. He didn't say anything because she had a habit of turning red whenever a compliment was paid to her.

Instead he said, "Comfy?"

"As a matter of fact, yes I am. I wish I could do my job in yoga pants."

"Really is nowhere to stash a gun though," he observed.

"No, there really isn't, is there?"

She turned away in hopes he wouldn't see her face turn red yet again. She sure wished she could control her damn blushing. Her buzzer went off again; they looked at the monitor, and it was Brad. She buzzed him in and stood by the door waiting for him to come up. When he came in, he went directly over to where Nathan was, said hi, and asked him to show him the footage. While they watched, Brad was asking questions and, once he was all filled in, said he would try to find out who purchased that handle and where it was purchased from.

"I'm going to ask around this neighborhood first, it may have been something he bought as an afterthought once he got here. He's got to know about the beefed-up security, or he wouldn't be worrying about being seen on the camera. I think it's time we put out a message that he should not be messing around with my stepdaughter."

"What are you going to do, Brad?" Sarah asked.

"I'm going to talk to the captain and see if we can issue some sort of press release and see what happens. I'll let you know once I talk to him in the morning. This guy is getting out of hand, and it's pissing me off. Your mom wants to know if you want to come and stay over tonight too."

"If it's ok with you, I think I will. My car is at the station because it wouldn't start. Nathan convinced me it was a good idea to go out to dinner so I could relax, which I did, but when we came back here, the damn buzzer was ringing before I even unlocked the door. He's got to be watching the place, how else would he know to stay out of sight and when I got home? He's making me crazy. I've been wracking my brain to try to figure out who would do this to me, and the only person I come up with is in jail. I'll go grab some clothes and ride over with you, if that's ok, Brad? Then I can ride with you to work in the morning."

"That's a good plan."

Sarah's phone chimed, and it was a text from her mom asking her if she wanted to come and stay overnight. She smiled and answered her yes, she'd be coming over with Brad.

Her mom texted her back, saying, "Good, then you can tell me about the date."

She let that one go unanswered.

22

What the hell? What was he doing here? Why was she in the car with him? Did they go on a date? How in the world was he ever going to get close to her? He seized the opportunity to interrupt their night when he pushed her buzzer. *I hope they look for me all night and it ruins whatever plans that dude may have had. I know what plans I would have for Sarah.* He fantasized about it as he drove away, not wanting to be around when the cops showed up.

Jim watched a guy who was dressed all in black, including a black hoodie that was pulled up so it was covering his head and face, walk up to the building, use a pole or something long to push a buzzer, and then get in his car and drive away. He thought this was suspicious, so he pulled out from his parking spot to follow him. He called dispatch to see if they would run the plates. When they got back to him, they told him that the license plate was registered to a car rental company and asked if he wanted the address.

"No, I'll just follow him to see where he goes."

He told them the coordinates he was currently at and what direction they were heading. He followed the car a couple of car lengths back so he wouldn't be spotted. The car started to speed up, and Jim thought that maybe the guy had made him, but it was just to get through a yellow light. Damn, the car flew through the light, and he was stuck three cars behind. The light turned green; he turned around and headed back to Sarah's. He radioed in that he lost the car and was heading back to Sarah's place. When he got to Sarah's, he noticed that Brad, Sarah, and some other guy were all out on the sidewalk talking. He parked and joined them.

"Hey, Detective, Sarah," Jim said. "I just followed some guy that pushed a buzzer with a pole, but I lost him. He was driving a car that is registered to a car rental agency, and when I was following him, he went through a yellow light, and I lost him."

"Really?" Sarah asked. "Did you get a good look at his face? What was he driving? Where was he headed when you lost him?"

"He was headed out of town toward Paradise, and no, I didn't see his face. He was wearing all black, including a hoodie that he had pulled up so it obscured his face."

"Damn, damn, damn!"

"I'm really sorry, I tried to hang back so he wouldn't see me, but then he went through the light and I was too far behind to catch him."

"It's ok, Jim, I know you did your best, and you were right to follow him. We'll follow up with the rental company in the morning," Brad reassured him.

"Thanks, Detective Hastings. Again, I'm sorry that I lost him," Jim said, and he walked back to his car to continue with his surveillance. Brad walked over to his car and let him know that Sarah would be at their house tonight but he still wanted him there to see if the guy showed up again.

23

Brad and Sarah rode over to his house in silence. Once they reached his house, Sarah said, "Sorry, I'm not very good company tonight, Brad."

"It's ok, sweetie. I understand. I was really hoping that this guy would get frustrated with the beefed-up security at your place, but I see he's finding ways around it."

"Whoever this creep is sure is pissing me off! I just want to know who and why. Why me again? Wasn't what happened to me years ago enough? I really don't want to go to a safe house because then I can't tell anyone where I am, I can't work, I can't have a life, and I don't want that at all. He hasn't shown signs of violence, so I'm going to stay in my apartment. I don't want any guff from you or mom, so just save the speech. I'm not a little kid anymore, and I will not stop living my life because someone is trying to scare me."

"I wouldn't dream of telling you what to do, Sarah. Your mom might, but I won't. Maybe instead of going to a safe house, you could go to your dad's for a little vacation? Since you'd be out of town, maybe this guy will give up or ramp up and make a mistake since he can't find you. We shouldn't tell anyone either except, of course, the captain and your mom. What do you think about that idea?"

"I don't want to run from this, I want to stay and fight and catch this guy, but going to my dad's might not be the worst idea ever. I'll think about it and make my decision in a couple of days. Thanks, Brad, for being there for me again!"

"Anytime, Sarah. You know, you disappearing might make more than one person anxious. What about Nathan?"

"Well, if no one is supposed to know, I can't really tell him now, can I? I hope he won't think it has anything to do with him if I do decide to leave. If you see him, maybe you could tell him?"

"I could, but I really think since we don't know who it is, we really need to keep this to ourselves."

"He's going to call me to find out where I am, that's if I go at all."

"I think it would be a wonderful idea for you to go spend some time with your dad and get away from this place and all this," he said as he waved his hand in a big circle.

"You may be right. I'll at least sleep on it and see how I feel in the morning."

They walked into the house where Lynda was waiting with steaming cups of hot cocoa.

"Come sit by me, honey, and tell me what's been happening."

Sarah and Brad sat in the living room with Lynda and recounted what had transpired that evening. Sarah also told her all about the other things that had been happening too so that her mom was up to speed.

"Oh my goodness, sweetheart, I had no idea all this was going on, why didn't you tell me?"

"I can handle it, Mom, I *am* a police officer. He just needs to make one mistake, and we'll catch him. Brad thinks that I should go spend some time with Dad to see if it makes this guy upset and he does something to get caught."

"I think that's a wonderful idea. What do you think?"

"I'm going to sleep on it and decide in the morning."

"What about the date you had this evening? What will he think?"

"Nathan? He's a tech at the station, and if he calls me, I'll just let him know that I am out of town for a little while, or I won't tell him anything. I don't know. I need to sleep on it and decide tomorrow. Since we aren't sure who it is, I want to tell as few people as possible. If it turns out to be the guy I'm interested in again, I'll swear off of men for the rest of my life!"

"Oh, honey, let's not go there unless we need to. Why don't you go upstairs and get some rest. We'll talk more tomorrow."

"You're right, Mom. I'll see you in the morning. Good night."

"Good night," Lynda and Brad said together.

Once Sarah went up to bed, Lynda said, "What are the chances it's this Nathan that she's talking about?"

"I'm sure it's not. He was in the apartment with her when the buzzer was pushed, and that guy drove away with one of our guys tailing him but lost him at a light. We've had round-the-clock surveillance at her apartment, and this guy just doesn't do enough for us to catch him. It's getting frustrating."

"I'm sure it is. I'm just glad you're sure it's not Nathan. I'm happy that she's actually gone out on a date. Are you going to continue to watch her place if she leaves?"

"Absolutely. If she's gone and there's no one for this guy to harass, maybe he'll make a mistake and we can catch him. They got a plate number tonight, but turns out it's for a car rental company. They are going to find out who rented the car and try to track him that way. We just need to get this guy so that Sarah can concentrate on herself and not someone stalking her. I'll talk to the captain in the morning to see if we can put someone in her apartment if she goes so that if her stalker decides to break in, we can grab him there."

"I just want this all to be over for her. That poor girl has had enough trauma in her life already. Thank you for always being there for her. It really means a lot to me, and I know Sarah appreciates it a great deal as well. I love you, Brad."

"And I love you. Let's go to bed, it's late, and we've both got early days tomorrow."

They locked up and headed up to bed.

24

About two in the morning, there was a loud banging on their door.

The doorbell was pushed repeatedly until Brad yelled down the stairs, "Hold on to your horses, I'm coming!"

When he reached the door, he looked through the side window and saw that it was Jim, one of the officers that was assigned to Sarah's apartment. Brad swung the door open. "What's going on? Why are you here so late and not at the apartment?"

"Sorry, I know it's late, sir, but we caught him! I wanted to come over and tell you myself right away so that Sarah will know she doesn't have to worry about him anymore."

Sarah was coming down the stairs when she heard the news and said excitedly, "Really? You caught him? Who was it? Why was he doing it?"

"Hold on, take it easy, Sarah," Brad said. "Let's all go in to the living room, and Jim can tell us what he knows."

Lynda had come down the stairs too and offered coffee or hot cocoa to anyone who wanted some. They all declined, wanting to hear what happened.

"Well, to start off with," Jim said, "his name is William Clover. He was pulled over a few months ago for a traffic violation by, you guessed it, Sarah. I saw him trying to get into the building, but no one was buzzing him in. When I approached him and asked him what he was doing, he tried to run past me, but I blocked his path. I asked him who he was trying to get in to see so badly, and at first he said no one, and as I pressed, he said Sarah, so I thought this *must* be the guy. I brought him to the station, and he's there, waiting to be interviewed. That's why I came over here, as lead detective, Brad, I thought you'd like to know right away."

"That is the best news I've heard in a long time!" Sarah said with a smile on her face that went from ear to ear.

"I'll second that!" her mom beamed back.

"Ok, I guess I better get changed and down to the station."

"I'm coming with you, Brad." Sarah held up her hand when he tried to protest. "No, I want to hear what this nut job has to say, and I want to hear it from his own mouth. I will sit in the observation room, and I won't make a peep, I promise."

"All right, Sarah, get changed, and you can come with me."

They all thanked Jim, he said goodbye, and Brad and Sarah went up to change.

Once at the station, Brad told the jailer to bring the guy to the second interrogation room and that he'd be right in. Sarah set up in the observation room to find out why this guy had it in for her. Brad entered the interrogation room with a file in his hand, threw it on the table, and after reading him his rights said, "Mr. Clover, care to tell me what you were doing this evening?"

"I wasn't doing anything."

"You were caught trying to get into a secured building that you don't live in and had no business going in to. Who were you there to see, and why wouldn't they let you in?"

"I was just trying to find a place to sleep for the night."

"Oh, c'mon, Bill, we both know that's not true. You told the officer that arrested you that you were there to see Sarah. Why were you there to see her?"

"I just picked a name off of the mailboxes to see if anyone would let me in so I could be warm and get some rest."

"You told the officer that Sarah pulled you over not long ago. How did you know where she lived? Have you been stalking her?"

"I don't know anyone named Sarah! Leave me the fuck alone."

"We both know that I can't do that. Tell me what you were doing, and we'll see what we can do about letting you get some rest."

"I'm not talking to you. I'm not going to talk to anyone, I'm done."

HE'S WATCHING

Brad tried other questions, but Bill just sat there looking at him with a glazed look in his eyes and wouldn't speak. Sarah was getting frustrated in the observation room but knew she couldn't go in there and confront him unless Brad said it was ok. After several more attempts, Brad walked out and went into the observation room that Sarah was in.

"Well, he isn't very forthcoming with answers, is he? Do you recognize him?"

"Yeah, I pulled him over a couple of months ago for speeding and running a red. Can I go in there and talk to him? I can confront him and see if he will tell me why he is doing this to me."

"I don't like that idea at all."

"What's he going to do to me? He's at the station, and you'll be watching from in here so, I think I'll be fine."

"Well, we really have nothing to lose, I guess. Sure, go ahead and go in there and talk to him. Maybe he will tell *you* why he's been harassing you."

"Thanks, Brad!" She threw her arms around him, giving him a big hug and a kiss on the cheek.

"Aw, go on, get in there and nail this bastard."

"Yes, sir!"

Sarah went into the interrogation room with the same folder that Brad had when he walked out. When the door opened, Bill's eyes almost popped out of their sockets.

"Wh-wh-what are you doing here" he stammered.

"I'm here to find out why you've been stalking me, how you knew where I lived, and what you had planned to do with me once you got to me. I suggest you start talking."

He seemed to recover a little when he said, "I didn't do anything to you."

"You didn't only because you didn't get the chance. Why me? What on earth did I do to you to make you want to hurt me?"

"You pulled me over, and I had a perfect record before that. Now I have to pay hundreds of dollars in fines, and my license will be suspended for a year, thanks to you!" he shouted at her.

"I was doing my job. If you hadn't been breaking the law, you wouldn't have gotten pulled over. Don't try to make me the bad guy here, Bill. You break the law and get caught, you have to pay for it."

"You're a bitch like all the rest of 'em."

"Who else are you talking about?"

"Women in general. I wish I had just broken down your door and beat the crap out of you. I wouldn't be having this conversation right now because you'd be in the hospital."

"That sounds very much like a threat, Mr. Clover. Threatening a police officer isn't taken lightly. You're already paying for traffic violations, why don't we add this to your list of offenses? Maybe instead of losing your license, you go to jail for a while so you can think about what you've done and what you *wanted* to do."

"Fuck you!" He lunged at her, and she throat-punched him. He crumbled to the ground, writhing in pain.

"Mr. Clover, you will have additional charges filed against you, and you *will* do jail time now. If you had just left well enough alone, you wouldn't be in this predicament."

He didn't speak only because he couldn't. There were tears coming out of his eyes as he looked up at her and gave her the finger.

"Very good, I'll have an officer take you back to your cell. You'll be booked tonight on a whole host of charges. Have a nice day, Bill."

Brad came out of the observation room, went into the interrogation room, pulled Bill to his feet and read off a list of new charges. He was taken back by one of the officers and placed in a cell.

"That went better than I had hoped," Sarah said.

"Are you kidding me? When he tried to attack you, I was almost out the door until I saw you throat-punch him. That was stellar," he chuckled. "Nice work, Wheeler!"

"Thanks. I knew I could handle it. I don't take all those self-defense classes for nothing. I suppose I will go write up my report on this."

"Sounds like a plan. I'm going to do mine too. Hey, have you heard yet about your promotional exam?"

"No, nothing yet. Kind of bums me out, but I know it can take weeks to find out."

"You'll hear soon enough, I'm sure."

"Say, Brad? Did you guys ever find out how Amy Stone died?"

"Oh yeah, seems she was out sunning herself and had a massive coronary. We had to break the news to her husband, and he took it really hard. He said that even though she was having an affair, he still loved her with all his heart and that he might as well be dead too. He is being transferred somewhere that will better be able to handle his depression."

"Wow, a heart attack? She wasn't that old, was she?"

"In her late 30's, I'd guess. Why, what are you thinking?"

"It just seems weird that she would be lying in the sun and then die of a heart attack. She wasn't that old, she wasn't overweight, and she didn't work. Could she have been given something that would have caused her to have a heart attack?"

"Well, the coroner said it was a heart attack, and she would know. I don't know if anything else was ruled out because it didn't look like foul play had a hand in it."

"Maybe you could ask her? It just seems odd to me."

"You know, you're going to make a great detective. I'll call her when I get to my desk and leave her a message to see if she thought about foul play. Now get going and get that report done."

"Thanks for checking on that, Brad. I'm on it. I'll have it done in a flash." She went and worked on the paperwork for her case. It was finally over, what a relief. She was going to let Nathan know so that he could come over and remove some of the unnecessary items. She was going to keep a few items just to be on the safe side.

25

Once her report was done, around seven o'clock, she decided to head out for some breakfast when her new partner, Shane, called out to her, "Hey, Sarah, where ya goin'?"

"Out for some breakfast. Wanna come?"

"Sure, I have our assignment for today too."

"Ok great. You probably don't know, we caught the guy that's been terrorizing me."

"Really, that's wonderful! When?"

"Early this morning. We came in around three o'clock and finally got him to talk. Brad let me in to talk to him, and he pretty much snapped, came after me, and I defended myself. He is in jail now with a whole bunch of charges and a sore throat."

"What was his reason for stalking you, and why a sore throat?"

She filled him in on everything that Bill had told her while they walked out to the car. They went to the Morning Thunder Café, ordered the special of the day, and discussed plans for the day.

"Well, let's get to it," she said when they finished breakfast.

"Ok, let's roll."

Shane drove and Sarah pulled out her phone to text Nathan that they caught the guy and that she'd like for him to come over and take out some of the security stuff in her apartment. He responded with a phone call.

"Hello?"

"Hey, it's Nate. You really caught the guy? That's fantastic, but how? Last time I saw you, Brad was taking you to your mom's and you weren't going to be home. He didn't follow you guys to your mom's, did he?"

"Slow down, I'll tell you everything."

She retold the story again. He was thrilled that she wasn't going to need the extra security but a little bummed that he might not see her as often. When she finished telling him everything, he asked if he could come over that night and take the equipment out of her apartment.

"Sure, that would be great. I'll even make dinner for us if you want."

"That would be nice, should I bring wine or the fixings for Mojito's?"

"How about a bottle of chardonnay? I can make some salmon and fingerling potatoes. How does six thirty sound?"

"Sounds like a date." She smiled as she hung up, and Shane looked at her and noticed that her face was pink.

"Date? I thought you didn't date?"

"I haven't much in my past, but I've been spending time with Nathan, and he's really a nice guy. He works for the police department, so I know that they've done a background check on him and if it wasn't clean, he wouldn't be there."

"Very nice. I'm glad for you."

"Thanks."

The rest of the day went by quickly, and when they were getting ready to head out, she remembered that her car didn't start the day before.

"Oh, damn!"

"What is it?" asked Shane.

"I forgot that my car didn't start yesterday, and I haven't done anything to fix it."

"I can give you a lift home if you'd like?"

"Oh, would you? That would be great. I have to stop at the market on the way home, is that ok?"

"Sure, that's fine. Are you ready to leave?"

"I'm ready if you are."

They left the station, stopped at the Save Mart, and Shane dropped her off at home.

"Enjoy your evening. Don't do anything I wouldn't do," he said with a wink when she was getting out.

"Oh, I'm sure I won't. Thanks for the lift, see you tomorrow."

26

She let herself in the front door and up to her apartment. She dropped the bags on the counter in the kitchen, decided to meal prep now, and then go up for a shower before Nathan got there. She was cutting things up for a salad when her cell chirped. It was a text message from her mom asking her if she wanted to come over for a celebration dinner. She texted her back thanking her but declined because she had another date with Nathan. Once everything was ready for dinner, she hopped in the shower and got ready for her date. She left her hair down and put on some yoga pants and a loose top. Her buzzer went off about six fifteen. *Early, I like that in a man*, she thought. She buzzed him up, waited by the door, and when she saw him, opened the door.

"Hi there," she said.

"Hi yourself. You look amazing."

Her face turned bright red, and she grabbed his hand and pulled him into the apartment, shut and locked the door, and planted a big kiss on his lips.

He returned the kiss but said, "You better stop that right now, young lady, or dinner isn't going to happen on time."

"What if I told you that it will be ready in about twenty minutes?"

"I'd say, let's crack open this bottle of wine and let it breathe while we decide what equipment I'm taking out of here."

"That's no fun, but you're right, we should do that now."

They talked about what was overkill and what made sense. He took the monitors and all the cameras but left the rest of it in place.

No sense in changing out a perfectly good lock. She could probably take the alarm off of her door though. Once that was finished, she told him it was time to eat. They ate at the kitchen table enjoying a glass of wine with dinner.

"Hey, this is really good, Sarah. You're a great cook."

"Thanks. I learned at a young age, I love to cook."

"Well, that might not be a good thing."

"Why is that?"

"If you cook for me too much, I'll get fat."

"Oh, come on now. You don't look like the kind of person that would get fat. Besides, we can always find some way to work off extra calories."

"Are you flirting with me?"

"No, I'm talking about joining a gym," she said sarcastically.

"Well, just what did you have in mind for burning extra calories?"

"Running around the block? Tennis? Either of those sound good?"

"No, I'll tell you what sounds good." He leaned over and whispered into her ear. Her face started to burn until it was beet-red.

"Stop that right now, you Neanderthal."

He laughed at her, and then she laughed too. They finished up dinner, did the dishes, and were sitting on the couch enjoying another glass of wine when he said, "I was serious before, about what I whispered into your ear."

"Oh, were you? Well, I can honestly say that I don't even know what some of that is. I'm…ah…oh, never mind."

"What is it, Sarah?" he asked concerned.

"It's really nothing, I…ah…haven't you know."

"Haven't what?"

"Haven't you know, had sex."

"Seriously? I know you said you didn't date a lot, but I didn't know that you were a virgin."

"Well, I am, and I'm a little embarrassed about it," she said with her face burning.

"Why? I think it's fantastic. You have no preconceived notions about what it might be like, do you?"

"Like what? Like it hurts or it's the best thing since sliced bread? I've heard things, but I have no idea what to expect."

"I can show you," he asked hopefully.

"I bet you could, but I just don't think I'm ready right now."

"Ok, I totally understand. Would you go out of town with me this weekend?"

"I think I can arrange that."

"Great. I'll take you anywhere you want to go."

"I'd like to go to Vegas. I've never been, and I think it would be a hoot."

"A hoot? If you're prepared to stay up all weekend and party like a rock star all night long, then yes, it's a hoot."

"Want to watch a movie?"

"I would love to, but it's getting late, and we both have to be up early."

"Oh, all right, I guess you're right. Thank you for everything that you've done to help bring me peace of mind. I really appreciate all of it."

"My pleasure. I'll haul this stuff down to the car and be back up in a few minutes."

"Don't be silly, I'll help you."

"No, you stay here, and I'll be back up in a few. I want a good night kiss."

"Ulterior motives, I see. Ok, I'll wait here."

Nathan came back up a few moments later, pulled her up from the couch, and gently kissed her lips. She parted them slightly, and he teased her lips with his tongue. She let out a sigh and a soft moan. He pushed his tongue into her mouth. She returned his hungry kiss. Her legs turned into Jell-O, so she had to cling to him. His kisses grew in intensity with Sarah responding to each one, so much so that she was ready to take him to her bedroom and he *could* show her what he meant when he whispered in her ear. He reluctantly pulled away from her, and she cried out a little when she asked why.

They were both breathing hard when he said, "Aw, Sarah, we better stop before things go too far."

They stood there holding each other waiting for their breathing to be normal again.

"Shit, I'm sorry. I don't want you to think that I'm a tease. I was almost ready to ask you if you wanted to go to my room."

"I don't think you're a tease, far from it. I really want your first time to be special, so I wouldn't feel right taking you to bed unless it's something that you really want."

"Right now I do. But you might be right. Damn it! I don't like that you're right about this."

"I don't want you to feel taken advantage of, that's the last thing that I would do to you. I hope you know that."

"If I didn't before, I do now. Thank you for coming over to get your equipment and having dinner with me."

"I'd be here every day if you needed or wanted me to be. Look, Sarah, I like you, and I want to keep on seeing you. You're beautiful, funny, smart, and can take care of yourself. I love it when you blush, and I love it when you're a hard ass. Do you really want to go out of town this weekend?"

"I do."

"Are we sharing a room?"

"We are."

"May I make a suggestion?"

"What about?"

"Let's go to Reno. It's only about three hours, and it would take us almost ten to get to Vegas. If you agree, I'll make all the arrangements."

"Ok, Nate, go ahead and make plans. I'll go to Reno with you, I've never been there either."

"Really, you'll go? Awesome, you won't regret it, I promise. We will have so much fun."

"Guaranteed?"

"Well, at least as much fun as you can have with your clothes on." He laughed when her head jerked up to look at him.

"I hope you're right because I'm going to hold you to it."

"Ok. Be ready Friday at about four thirty. I'll pick you up, and we'll take my car."

"Oh shit!"

"What?"

"I forgot about my car. It's still at the station and wouldn't start. I don't suppose you know anything about cars?"

"Not a thing. I do think you need a new one though. Want to go car shopping tomorrow night after work? I can bring you home if you don't find anything."

"Really? Nate, you surprise me more and more. Yes, let's go look at new cars for me. This is very exciting. I haven't bought a new car before."

"It's about time that you do then. You deserve it. You've had some pretty awful shit happen in your life, and you deserve to do what makes you happy."

"You are right, about all of it. Thanks, Nate, again for everything."

"You're welcome, Sarah, for everything. I'll see you tomorrow after work." He leaned down and kissed her long and slow.

She didn't want to let go when he pulled away, and she said, "I wish you wouldn't go."

"It's better this way, at least right now."

"Ok, good night, Nate."

"Good night, Sarah." He blew her a kiss at the door.

27

The next morning when Sarah got to work, Captain Layton called her into his office and shut the door.

Oh crap, she thought, *this can't be good*.

"Sarah, have a seat. I wanted you to come in this morning because I wanted to discuss a few things with you. First, that guy that got shot at the plaza, Robert Stone, will make a full recovery. He's in a hospital that can help with his wound and his depression. It looks like it might be a long road of recovery for him. He is going to have to do some time for his actions, but that's to be expected. The coroner confirmed that his wife did, indeed, have a heart attack, ruling out any signs of foul play, so case solved. As far as your case goes, everything is getting buttoned up, and he will be in jail for a while. I wasn't too happy with Brad letting you talk to your stalker, but at least you got him to admit what he's done, and the throat punch was epic," he said with a big smile on his face. "Finally, your exam results came."

Her eyes widened as she waited. He was shuffling papers around on her new desk, and she finally said, "Well, did I pass?"

"You passed with flying colors. Congratulations, Detective Wheeler!" he said as he presented her with her new nameplate for her desk.

"Oh my god, are you kidding me? I did it? I did it! This is one of the best days of my life!" she said as she was getting up about to leave his office.

"Hold on there, Wheeler. You are going to be assigned a partner."

"Aw, come on, Captain," she said a little irritated.

HE'S WATCHING

"No arguments!"

Just then, someone knocked on the door.

"Come in," barked the captain.

"Hi, you wanted to see me as soon as I got here?" Brad asked.

"Yes, have a seat, Brad. I was just going over some things with Sarah. I congratulated her on becoming a detective and also told her that she's going to need a partner."

"Congrats, Sarah! I knew you could do it."

"Thanks, but I don't need a partner."

"All our detectives have partners, like it or not, that's the way it is. Brad, will you talk to her? She doesn't listen to reason."

"Sure. Sarah, listen, we all work with partners, someone to have your back and all that. What the captain is trying to tell you is that I will be your partner."

"What? No, oh my god, this is great! We work well together, and I know you always have my back! And I will always have yours! Thank you, Captain!"

"Don't thank me, he offered to do it, and I jumped at the chance for you to learn from one of our seasoned vets. Make me proud, Detective."

"I will do my best. I can't wait to tell Mom. Is that all, Captain?"

"Yeah, Wheeler, get out of here."

"Wait for me at my desk though, Sarah, we're going to put you at a desk by mine."

"Ok, I'm just going to go call Mom."

She left the office while Brad and the captain talked. She went to Brad's desk, sat down, and called her mom. For once, her mom answered her phone.

"Hello, sweetie, to what to I owe the honor of a phone call?"

"Well, I have some news."

"Oh? I have a few minutes before my next showing, did you want to share your news?"

"I do want to share. I passed my exam, Mom, I'm a detective!" she blurted out.

"What? That's fabulous, honey, what great news!"

"Oh, there's more news. Brad and I are going to be partners."

"Oh, that's just the best news ever. At least I know you will be watching out for one another out there."

"Yes, I'm so excited, I can't believe it. Nate is taking me car shopping tonight too. Mine's been dead for a few days."

"Well, what a wonderful way to celebrate. You've been seeing a lot of this Nate?"

"Not a lot, he installed all my surveillance equipment, and we got to know each other a little bit, and now we've been on a couple dates, but I do like him. Can you believe I said that?"

"I knew it would take someone special to break down that wall of yours. Oh, sweetheart, I'm so very happy for you, but I have to run. We'll talk soon."

"Ok, Mom, bye."

"Goodbye and congratulations."

28

Sarah was going to wait to tell Nate but thought he might hear about it from someone, so she texted him to call her if he was free. He texted back and asked where she was. She said by Brad's desk, and he said he'd be right up. She was looking for him when he walked into the squad room. She got a huge smile on her face, walked over to him, hugged him, and said, "I've got some pretty terrific news to share."

"Hi, that was a nice surprise. What's the news?"

"I made detective, and Brad is going to be my partner."

"Oh, Sarah, that's fantastic. I'm so proud of you."

"Thanks! I'm over the moon. We should celebrate."

"We can celebrate this weekend in Reno."

"We could too, couldn't we? A new car, a weekend getaway, we caught the jerk stalking me, I have a man in my life, and I have the job that I've wanted for almost eight years. This is one of the best days of my life."

"I couldn't be happier for you. How about dinner tonight? Before or after car shopping makes no difference to me."

"How about after? Then we will have one more thing to celebrate if I find one."

"That sounds like a perfect idea. Do you know what you want to look at?"

"I really don't. Did you research cars before you bought yours?"

"I did, and the Rav is one of the few that I liked."

"Would you show me the others you didn't like? I usually just buy one I think will last for a few years, but I really need to have reliable transportation since I'm going to be a detective now. I really like the sound of that, Detective Wheeler."

"I like it too. I've got to get back to work, but I'll meet you back up here at about four thirty?"

"That should work, at least it does right now."

"Cool, I'll see you later."

"Later, Nate."

Brad was walking over when he saw Nate leaving. "Did you tell him?"

"I sure did, and I called and told Mom too. They are both very happy for me."

"I'm very proud of you, Sarah. I knew you could do it. Let's get your desk all set up, and then if nothing comes up, we'll start on the cases I'm working on, how does that sound?"

"It sounds great."

They cleaned out the desk that was directly across from Brad. Brad's old partner had been there, but he had moved, and Brad had been without a partner for a few months.

Sarah looked at Brad and asked him, "Was it your idea to be partners with me?"

"It was actually the captain's idea. I agreed because we both needed a partner, and I know how hard you work. There might even be some things that you can see about my current cases that I'm missing. Fresh, young eyes to look things over from a new perspective could be just what I need to solve some of these."

"I'd love to look at your case files. Can I take them home to study them?"

"You can. Let's get everything squared away here first, and then we'll talk more about them."

"Ok."

They got the desk cleaned out of the items that she wouldn't need. She moved things around on the desk to make it more functional and placed her name placard on her desk when they were finished.

"How does it look, Brad?"

"It looks like it was meant to be there. Ok, here are the files I have right now. Some of them are old, cold case files I thought I'd try to work on. Others are ones that I can't get the victims or perps to talk about. You go ahead and look them over, and if you have some ideas, write them down, and we can go over them, ok?"

"Yep, sounds like a plan. Is it time for lunch yet?"

"Would you look at that, it is. Let's go grab a bite."

They left for lunch, grabbed some fast food, and went to the plaza to eat. It was a beautiful sunny day in early June. They sat in the plaza enjoying the sunshine and watching the people bustling about.

"It sure is gorgeous today," Sarah commented.

"It really is. One of those days I'd like to play hooky."

"You don't do such things, do you, Brad?"

"Not very often, but once in a while. You can't work all of the time, that's why they offer paid time off, so you don't get burned out."

"I don't think I'll ever get tired of being a detective."

Brad chuckled when he said, "It's your first day, but just wait, once you've been doing it for as long as I have, you'll get tired of it sometimes."

"Maybe, but I've enjoyed the last several years of my life being a cop. I feel like I have a purpose, that I'm needed, and I really like that."

"You're a great person, Sarah, don't let anyone take advantage of that."

"What do you mean?"

"Just that, you like to help out, and if I wasn't your partner, some of the other 'dicks' might take advantage of how hard you work, and I would really hate for that to happen to you."

"Well, partner, that won't happen. I have a feeling we'll be partners for a very long time."

"At least a year, if I can stand you," he joked with her.

"You'll be lucky to have me as a partner for a year. Watch your manners, or you'll have to get a new one sooner than you'd like," she joked back.

They finished up their lunch, got back in the car, and headed back to the station.

Once inside, Brad handed her a stack of about fifteen files.

"These are all of your case files?"

"Not all of them are mine, some of them are cold cases, and we all share in working cold cases."

"Ok, but shouldn't we concentrate on the newer ones first?"

"Yes, we should, but if you're taking some home, why not take the old ones, you might see something that will bust the thing wide open. We can work on the current ones while we are here. How does that sound?"

"Sounds like a plan. I'll take these home, but I won't take them until I can look at them."

"Ok, lock them up before you leave today. Oh, did you ever get your car fixed?"

"No, Nate and I are going car shopping and for dinner after work."

"A third date? This sounds serious."

"It's not serious yet. I do really like him though, and I know he likes me."

"I'm very happy for you, Sarah. You seem a lot more relaxed than normal, and it's good to see you let your hair down, so to speak."

"Thanks, Brad. I guess things are going pretty great for me. Oh, I should tell my dad." She grabbed her cell and called her dad.

"Hello, this is Glenn."

"Hi, Dad, it's me."

"Sarah, honey, it's good to hear your voice. What's going on, is everything ok?"

"Yes, things are great, Dad. I have something to tell you."

"What is it?"

"I made detective today, Dad. Brad is going to be my partner."

"Oh, sweetie, that's marvelous! I'm very happy for you, and I must say I'm even happier that Brad will be your partner. Someone to watch out for my baby."

"Ah, Dad, I can take care of myself. But I'm really happy too."

"When are you coming for a visit? It seems like it's been forever."

"I'll come soon. Maybe next weekend or the weekend after?"

"I'll check the calendar and let you know if we have anything pressing."

"Ok, Dad. I'll talk to you soon."

"Ok pumpkin. I love you."

"Love you too. Bye."

Blushing, she turned to Brad and said, "Parents," and shrugged.

He chuckled and said, "Yes, you're lucky to have two very special parents."

"And you, Brad, I have you too. You've been like a father to me too, and I love you."

He looked at her, looked away, cleared his throat, blinked rapidly, looked back at her with his eyes welled up with tears, and said, "Aw, damn, Sarah, I love you too. Just like you were my own kid."

They each laughed a little but seemed to come to the same conclusion. They each knew for sure that they could depend on the other to have their back no matter what happened.

29

She waited for Nate to come up at four thirty so they could go car shopping. He texted her he was on his way up. She shut down her computer, locked up the files, and went to meet him at the door. They walked out to his car in silence.

"Everything ok, babe?"

"Huh? Oh yeah, everything's ok. Did you just call me babe?"

He blushed this time and said, "Uh yeah, I did. Sorry."

"No, I like it. I was just lost in thought is all."

"I know, you seem a million miles away. What's up?"

"Just that Brad and I had a nice conversation earlier today, and I have a new respect for that man. We're going to be great partners."

"That's great. Hungry, or do you want to shop first?"

"Can we go to my place first so I can change?"

"Of course. You won't have to go home to change anymore, no more uniform."

"No more uniform, yippee! Where are we going shopping for cars?"

"Depends on what you want. Do you want a car or a SUV? Do you want new or used? Do you want a hybrid or gas? Do you want a stick or automatic?"

She cut him off, saying, "Ok, ok, let's talk about it over dinner, and then will you tell me where we are going to look?"

"Yes, then I will tell you what I think based on what you say."

"Ok. I'll just be a sec." She ran up, changed, and came back down, jumping in the car. "How fast was that?"

"It was longer than a sec, but not bad. What do you feel like for dinner?"

"Is this going to be twenty questions again?"

"No, you pick where you want to go."

"In that case, let's go to the 5th Street Steakhouse."

"Right on, I love it there, and I'm starved." She smiled at his enthusiasm.

When they arrived, they walked in, and the place was busy already.

"Oh, boy, it's getting packed in here. Want to sit at the bar?"

"Sure, makes no difference to me. I'm with the prettiest girl in the place tonight, you can lead me anywhere, and I'd follow you."

"Settled, bar it is."

They sat at the bar, looked over the menu, and ordered their dinners. They talked about what kind of car she was looking for and how excited she was to be a detective. They talked all the way through dinner, and she thought she knew what kind of car she was going to get. They drove to the Dodge dealership to look over the Challengers they had. She knew she wanted a fast car and figured she'd be able to catch anyone in that car. Besides, she loved the look, and with her new job came more money, but that was icing on the cake. She test-drove a few and liked what she was driving but decided to sleep on it and make her decision after talking to Brad.

"That was a blast," she exclaimed when they were leaving. "I love those Challengers. They're fast and sleek and just what I need if I ever get into a high-speed chase."

"Oh boy, just another reason for me to worry about you."

"Why would you worry about me?"

"Because, silly, I care about you." After a pause, he added, "A *lot*."

Her head was swimming. This seemed like it was going so fast. Did normal relationships work like this?

"I care about you as well, Nate."

"Enough to invite me up when we get to your house?"

"Not tonight. Only because I want to call Brad and talk to him about my choice of cars. He'll know better than I will if it's practical."

"Ok, fine, if that's the way you want to be." He pouted a little bit but then said, "I'm teasing, today has been a very exciting day for you, a new job, possible new car, new partner."

"New guy."

"Sorry what?"

"New guy in my life. That's been pretty exciting too."

"Thank you. I'm glad you said that. I really like being with you, and we have a lot of fun together. I'm really looking forward to this weekend."

"I am too. I haven't traveled much in my life."

"That's the only reason you're looking forward to it?"

"Well, no, I haven't gambled much in my life either." She was going to drag this out as long as she could, teasing him. She tried so hard to keep a straight face as he looked at her sideways while he drove.

"Just those two reasons?"

"Well, no, I haven't been in a town where there is night life all night long either."

"Anything else?"

"I haven't been alone with a guy all weekend long before either."

"That's the part I'm looking forward to, the being with you all weekend long. All those other people will mean nothing while I'm with you."

"You say the sweetest things. No wonder I'm always blushing when I'm with you. Do you do that on purpose? Say things to make me blush?"

"I can't help it if the truth makes you blush. Obviously, you haven't been given enough compliments in your life, but that's going to change. You can blush your heart out because I will continue to say nice things to you as long as you will let me." He pulled over to the side of the road in front of her building to let her out. She leaned over and gave him a nice, long kiss. "Good night, Nate. See you tomorrow."

"Good night, Sarah, see you tomorrow."

She literally floated up to her apartment, let herself in, and went in to take a hot shower before bed.

30

When she awoke the next morning, she checked her cell and saw that she had a few missed calls and a voice mail from her mom. Strange that she didn't hear it ring in the night. She looked at the phone and realized she had shut the ringer off when she was at dinner and never turned it back on. She listened to the voice mail and turned white as a sheet. She tried to call her mom back, but it went right to voice mail. She called the captain and started to tell him what his mother had said in her voice mail, but he already knew. He said there were already cops at the house and that she should go to the hospital to be there for her mother. She forgot, she didn't have a car. She called Nate and asked if he could come and get her right away and bring her to the hospital. He said he'd be right over. When he arrived, she jumped in the car, tears streaming down her face.

"Sarah, what is it? Why are we going to the hospital?"

"It's Brad," she said between sobs. "There was a break-in at their house last night, and he was beat up and shot, my mother found him when she came home from her showing. Please, God, don't let anything happen to Brad." She cried even harder.

"Honey, listen, the doctors are going to do all that they can for him. He lived through the night, so that's a good sign, right? I'll be with you as much as you want me to be, I won't let you go through this alone."

"It's not me I'm worried about, it's my mom. He is her whole world. He is one of the best people I know and has been a rock for our family since he came into our lives. I appreciate you driving me to the hospital too."

"It's no problem! I'll take you wherever you need to go."

"Thank you. Please let him make it God, please," she prayed. When they got to the hospital, she stopped at the desk to find out what room he was in.

"He is currently in surgery. Go all the way down this hall and take a right, go through the doors, and talk to the nurse at the desk, and they can give you more information."

"Thank you, c'mon, Nate, let's go."

"Right behind you."

They practically ran down the hall, found the nurses' station, and asked about Brad.

"Let's see, they took him back into surgery this morning when they felt he would be stronger. He lost a lot of blood, but he did survive the night so the doctors are hopeful."

"Do you know where his wife, my mother, is?"

"She may be in the waiting room or the chapel. I'm not sure."

"Thank you, I'll find her."

"I can page her if you can't find her, dear."

"Thank you, I'll let you know."

Sarah and Nate headed to the family waiting room. There was no one in there, so they headed toward the chapel. He mom was sitting in the front of the chapel, head bowed, softly crying.

"Mom?"

Lynda picked up her head, turned around, and saw Sarah and Nate. She stood up and started running toward her. Sarah ran to her mom, and they embraced and cried together.

"How are you holding up?"

"I'm doing ok, better now that you're here though. You must be Nate?"

"Oh, sorry, yes, this is Nate. Nate, this is my mother, Lynda."

"Very nice to meet you. I'm so sorry for what's happened. Can I get either of you anything?"

"Coffee?" Lynda requested.

"I'll be right back," he said and reached over and squeezed Sarah's hand.

"How is he, Mom? They said he went back into surgery this morning? Why did he have to go back in? Where are your clothes?"

"Oh, Sarah, it's awful. He was beaten so badly I couldn't tell if he was even breathing when I came in. He has a gunshot wound to his upper chest, and the bullet was close to puncturing his lung. They went in to remove the bullet, but there seemed to be internal bleeding as well, so they did what they could. There is so much blood in the house. I can't stop seeing it everywhere. I don't know what they used to beat him with, but there is even blood on the ceiling. I thought for sure he was dead when I found him. I'm so glad you're here, honey, I don't know what I'll do if I lose him. He's the best thing that's ever happened to me besides you. I love him so much. We were just talking about retiring early, in the next couple of years at least. My clothes are in the garbage, I imagine. When I got here, I was covered in blood, and they were nice enough to give me some scrubs to put on. How are you doing, sweetheart?" she asked through her tears.

"I'm ok. I'm just worried about Brad and you. You need to keep up your strength. When's the last time you ate anything?"

"Oh, one of the nurses brought me a muffin this morning, she told me the same exact thing."

"Do you want to pray together?"

"We haven't done that for a long time, have we?"

"No, but I think that we should. Come on."

She grabbed her mom's hand and led her back to the front of the chapel. They sat down, bowed their heads, and Sarah said, "God, I know we don't do this very much, at least not out loud, but I'm here with my mom, and Brad is in surgery fighting for his life. You already know all of this though. Please, God, please keep Brad safe. He has a lot to live for and a lot to look forward to. We love him very much, and"—her voice cracked but she pushed on—"I don't want him to miss out on one thing. He's the best thing that's ever happened to us, and we don't want to lose him. If I could do anything to help him, I would."

"You are, Sarah," the voice came from behind them.

They both turned to see Glenn and Nate standing in the door of the chapel. Both women stood up and walked toward the back of the chapel, each one trying to dry their eyes.

"It's ok to cry, you know," Glenn said as he held open his arms for either one of them.

Both of them went to him, started to cry all over again, and he hugged them fiercely. After about a minute, he said, "How is he, Lynda?"

"He's in surgery," she said after she pulled herself away.

Sarah gave her dad another squeeze and said, "Did you meet Nate, Dad?"

"Yes, as a matter of fact, I did."

Nate had set the coffees down but offered them to anyone; only Lynda accepted.

"Thanks, Nate. This should help warm me up."

"Did you sleep at all last night, Mom?"

"Not a wink. I'm tired and scared, and my emotions are all over the place."

"Do you have any idea who might have done it?"

"When I called 911, they sent detectives, an ambulance, and the captain showed up too. I don't know what they've found. I left in the ambulance and have been here ever since."

"Do you want me to go to the house and get you some clothes?"

"I don't even think they'll let you in yet. I can only imagine what they are doing to our house. They are probably tearing it apart room by room. It's going to be such a mess. Oh no, what time is it?" she asked panicked.

"It's about ten in the morning, why?"

"I have a showing at ten thirty. I'll have to cancel it, but I don't even think I have my phone with me. I left in such a rush I don't know if I stuck it back in my purse after I called 911. Now what am I going to do?"

"I'll call your office, Mom, and see if they can get someone else to go show it for you or ask one of them to call and cancel for you. I'll be back in a few minutes."

Nate followed her out of the chapel.

"So, Glenn, how did you know what happened?"

"Sarah texted me this morning after she listened to your message. I'm so sorry, Lynda. Is there anything that I can do for you?"

"Honestly?"

"Yes, honestly."

"Pray. I've been praying since I got here. I've hardly left this chapel."

"Of course I'll pray with you."

They went to the front of the chapel and sat together, praying silently to God to keep Brad safe.

31

When Sarah called her mom's office and told them what happened, they said, "Don't worry about a thing, we'll take care of everything." They had a copy of her day planner and said they'd get ahold of the guy she was supposed to show the house to and see if he still wanted to see it or if he wanted to wait until she was available. Sarah thanked them and hung up.

"Everything is all set for my mom, they said they'd take care of everything for her until she comes back."

"That's great news. What can I do for you? I feel so helpless, standing around doing nothing."

"I just thought of something, you need to go to work. I'm sorry, I didn't even think that you'd be missing work. I can catch a ride with Dad over to the house to get some things for my mom."

"Um, no, I'm not going to work. I called and told my boss this morning what was going on, and he told me to stick around here until you don't need me anymore."

"Well, if that's the case, will you be sticking around for a while then?"

"As long as you need me, babe." He gave her a big hug.

As they were walking back to the chapel, they heard one of the nurses at the desk ask if anyone knew where Mrs. Hastings was.

"I'm her daughter, she's in the chapel. Is everything ok?"

"Yes, dear, we just wanted to let her know that Mr. Hastings is being brought back from surgery."

"How is he? Is he going to make it?"

"I really can't discuss any of this with you, I'm sorry. Please have your mom come to the desk before she goes back to his room."

"Yeah sure," she said, a little annoyed that they wouldn't tell her how Brad was. "Why won't they tell me if he's going to be ok?"

"Maybe it's too soon to tell. It's a plus that he's going back to his room, isn't it?"

"I guess so."

They walked back into the chapel and saw her mom and dad in the front, and it looked like they were praying together.

"Mom?"

"What is it?" she said, trying to keep her voice even.

"The nurses at the desk said to please go to the desk, Brad's being brought back to his room, but you need to stop there before going to his room."

"Oh, thank God, let's go."

They all hurried to the desk, but the nurses wanted to have a private conversation with Lynda. She told them to go to Brad's room and she'd be in shortly. They went to his room where the three of them stood and talked quietly, wondering what the nurses had to say. When she walked into the room, there were fresh tears streaming down her face.

"Mom? What is it? Is Brad ok?"

"Oh, Sarah, I don't know. They've put him in a medically induced coma for at least the next twelve hours, maybe longer. I can't talk to him or hold him or anything."

"It must be for his own good, for his healing. You can still talk to him and hold him, he'll still hear you. At least that's what I believe. I don't know for sure, but it can't hurt for all of us to be here, so he knows we are all pulling for him."

Her mom's tears started to subside a little bit. "Do you really think so, honey?"

"I really do, Mom."

"Mrs. Hastings, my cousin was in a coma once, and our whole family was by his bedside, talking to him and telling him to get better, that we had a ton of things to still do and when he came out of it, he remembers hearing things while he was in the coma. For what it's worth, I think it will do a world of good."

"Oh, Nate, thank you for that. I suppose it wouldn't hurt. I just want this nightmare to be over. Who could have done this, and why?"

"Do you want me to call the captain and see if he has any ideas or if any of them do?"

"Oh, sweetheart, that would be nice, but I don't really know if I want to know at this point. I do, but I don't, ya know? I do because I'd like to kill them for doing this to all of us, and I don't because I don't want to accidentally tell Brad."

Glenn cleared his throat and said, "Sarah, walk with me for a minute?"

"Sure, Dad. I'll be right back, Mom."

She went into the hall with her dad, who said, "Listen, I feel like a third wheel here, I'm going to go home, but please tell your mother that Brad and she will both be in my prayers. I just had to come and let her know that I still care, and I'm here if you guys need me ok?"

"Thanks for coming, Dad, but I'm sure she'd like to thank you and say goodbye."

"Oh, honey, it's ok. Once this all blows over, I'd like all of us to get together and get to know one another. Your mom and I have both moved on, and you're a grown woman now, maybe we can all learn to be friends. I don't know how she'll feel about it, but if you want to mention it to her sometime, that would be ok with me."

"I think she might just like that. I know I would."

"Make sure and bring your Nate with you too."

"He's not really *my* Nate, we just started seeing each other, but I do like him a lot."

"He likes you a lot too," he said with his eyes twinkling. "Just bring him with. Give Brad my best when he wakes up. I love you, honey." He gave her a bear hug goodbye, and he left.

When Sarah went back into the room, her mom asked, "Where's your dad?"

"He said to tell you goodbye, that he gives his best to you and Brad, and that when this is all over, he'd like us all to get together and get to know one another and try to be friends. I told him you might just like that idea."

"We'll see what happens. Oh, here they come," she said as the nurse opened the door to wheel Brad in.

32

Brad was lying in the hospital bed with bandages wrapped around his head and covering most of his face. They had a number of different wires and tubes coming out of his body that were responsible for keeping him breathing. Sarah was in shock but tried to hide it. Brad didn't look very good at all; his skin was pale, and he looked small hooked up to all those machines and so many bandages.

"Hi, I'm Nurse Stevens. Mr. Hastings's internal bleeding has been repaired. He is in a medically induced coma to keep the swelling down on his brain and to give him some time to heal. Once he shows some signs of improving, the doctor will slowly bring him out of the coma. We will be feeding him through an IV. Do you have any questions?"

"Only about a hundred, but for now, I'll just see how everything works, and if I have any questions, I'll ask later on. Is it ok if I stay here with him overnight?"

"We don't allow visitors to stay in the room, but I'll check with the doctor to see if we can arrange something for you. I know this all looks scary and he was hurt very badly, but with enough time, rest, and love, he should get better."

"Oh, thank you so much. I'll sleep in the waiting room if I have to, I just want to be here in case he wakes up."

"He won't be waking up until the doctor reduces his medication to take him out of the coma. If you want to go home to sleep, it will do you a lot of good and in turn will do him a lot of good."

"I can't go home, my house is a crime scene."

"Oh my. Well, I'll talk to the doctor and see what he thinks we can do for you tonight."

"If she can't stay here, she can always come home with me and stay at my place," Sarah said.

"It's going to be a long time before Mr. Hastings is at hundred-percent. He was wounded pretty badly, as I stated before, but you won't do him any good if you are sick and can't help take care of him. I would suggest, for tonight at least, go stay with her and try to get as much sleep as possible. Leave phone numbers and everything with us so if anything at all happens, we can call and let you know."

"Thank you, Nurse Stevens. I'll see to it that my mom gets some rest."

"Ok then. It's still early. You can sit with him, talk to him, read to him, or whatever you'd like to do, he can still hear you, but I wouldn't tell him anything you don't want him to know." She winked as she walked out.

"She's a nice nurse," Sarah commented.

"Yes, they've all been wonderful, but I just hate the idea of not being here with him all night."

"You know exactly what he'd tell you too, right, Mom?"

"Yes, for god's sake, Lynda, go home and get some rest, I'll be fine until the morning."

"That sounded just like him." Sarah laughed. Lynda laughed a little bit too.

"Thanks for offering your house to me too, honey, it really means a lot. I'd rather stay here, but I know it would probably be better if I didn't. I just don't want something to happen to him while I'm gone."

"Well, she just told us that they won't wake him up so, let's just plan on you coming home with me tonight."

"Ok, fine, I will. I just remembered, I don't have a car."

"Neither do I, Nate drove. I was going to go buy a car today, but I think that will have to wait for a couple more days. I'm going to call the captain and see if I can take a couple more days off too. I'll be right back."

Sarah stepped into the hall to call her boss and to see if he had any news on who could have done this to Brad. When he answered, she asked if it was ok to take a few more days off.

He replied, "Take off as much time as you need. Hell of a thing that happened to him. How's he doing anyway?"

"They have him in a medically induced coma. Say, Cap, do they know who or why?"

"Damn! No, neither. If we can get to the who, we'll figure out the why. We have dusted for fingerprints in that whole house, but it's going to take a while to sort it all out and run them all through IAFIS."

"Shit, I was hoping that I could go to Mom's and get her some things to stay at my place."

"Get me a list, and one of the detectives will bring them to the hospital."

"She's going to need lady things that she won't be comfortable having someone else touch, if you know what I mean."

"Oh, all right, I'll meet you over there in twenty minutes."

"Ok, I'll be there."

Sarah walked back into Brad's room and motioned for Nate to come into the hall. "Will you bring me to my mom's? I want to go get some things for her, and the captain said to be there in twenty."

"Of course I will. Your mom just put her head down on the side of the bed, she might be sleeping."

"Good, she needs to rest. Let's run over there and pick some stuff up for her. This way, I can get a look at the crime scene too and see if I see anything someone else might have missed."

They started walking to the car.

"Honestly, Sarah? You're thinking about work at a time like this?"

"No, Cap said that they don't know who or why and that they've dusted the whole place. I know that house, I'll know if something is missing. I was just there a couple of days ago before they caught that creep that was stalking me. I can take a look around and let Layton know if I see something wrong. My mom certainly won't do it, and we know Brad can't, so I'm the logical choice." She started to feel better that she might be able to help instead of just sitting around the hospital crying and worrying why this happened.

When they reached the house, they headed to the front door and were opening it when a uniformed cop ran up and said, "Um, no one is allowed in there."

"I'm the owners' daughter, and I'm here to get some of my mother's things. Besides, Captain Layton told me I could come over here."

"I can't let you in there. No one has told me that anyone is allowed in there."

"Here comes the captain, he'll tell you I can go in."

"It's all right, Murphy, she can go in, I'm going in with her."

"Whatever you say, Cap."

"Thanks." To Sarah he said, "After you." To Nate he said, "You might want to stay out here."

"It's ok, Cap, he's with me."

"It's not a trust issue, it's a crime-scene issue. It's not a pretty scene in there, and we would rather not have too many people see it."

"You ok being out here, Nate?"

"Sure, no problem."

"Thanks, I won't be long."

"Take your time."

33

Sarah and the Captain walked in the front door, and Sarah was in utter disbelief at what she saw. The way her mom described it wasn't even close to what it actually looked like. This was after everything was done though, she had to remind herself. The place was a mess, chairs overturned, broken glass littered the floor, papers were strewn about, and the blood. There was blood everywhere, and it was starting to stink.

"Holy shit! What in the world happened in here? It looks like a bomb went off!"

"Well, from what the first officer on scene said, your mom was holding Brad's head in her lap, and she was covered in blood, EMT rushed over to him and started to work on him right away to try to stop the bleeding. I sure wish I knew who did this, I'll have their head on a silver platter when this is done."

"Yeah, Mom was in OR scrubs when I got to the hospital. She said the staff brought them to her and that her clothes may be in the garbage. Can I look around quick to see if I can tell if anything is missing? I know Mom won't come back in here to do that. Speaking of my mom, when will she be allowed back in? I don't want her to see any of this. I want to make sure the entire house is spotless before she comes back here. I don't even know if she'll want to continue to live here, she may want to sell it as soon as possible. I think that might depend on if Brad makes it or not. He's going to make it right, Cap? He's a strong man, and he's loved by so many, he just has to live. Besides, he's my new partner, and I'm not going to let him get out of that duty so easily." She had tears in her eyes as she talked about him.

"Wheeler, time will tell if he will pull through. All we can do right now is hope for the best."

"I know, I keep telling myself this is a hell of a nightmare that I'd like to wake up from at any time."

"You know the risks of being a cop. This, though, this is the worst kind of attack. Alone in your own home, minding your own business, and someone breaks in to try to kill you, over what? Once they leave, you're left fighting for your life, wishing that someone would come home and then hoping that they don't because you don't want them to get hurt too. I don't know, Wheeler. I don't know who would do this kind of sick, twisted crime. You go look around, grab the stuff your mom needs, and let's get out of here."

"Ok, but I'm going to tell you this right now. I'm going to figure out who did this to Brad, and I'll make them pay for it. They'll be in jail so long they're going to think they were born there. I'll be back in a few minutes."

She started at the door and looked around the room, trying to picture it in her mind the way it had looked before any of this had taken place. Where pictures used to hang, now there was empty space, except for blood smears in some spots. She went into each room and did the same thing, willing herself to not see it in its current state but as it was just a few short days ago. She went upstairs to get some of her mom's things. There wasn't as much disturbed up here, but things were not the way they should be either. She noticed that drawers had been pulled out and emptied wherever they decided to drop the stuff. What in the world were they looking for? She noticed it as soon as she opened the closet door in their bedroom. They had a safe built into the floor in the closet, and it held all their private papers and some cash. It looked like someone had tried to open the safe but didn't succeed; there were bullet holes, scratch marks, and some of the numbers were crushed like they had beaten *it* up too. *I wonder if CSI saw this.*

She called down the stairs, "Hey, Captain, do you know if any of the CSI guys were in their bedroom closet?

"I don't know for sure, why?"

"You might want to come up here and take a look." She heard him coming up the stairs. She pointed to the floor of the closet.

"Would you look at that," he said. "Looks like we might have just found motive."

"It isn't open. Do you think they will try to come back?"

"Hard to say, but I think we need to empty it if we can get it open."

"I don't know the combo, I only knew it was here, that's why I looked. Let me call my mom and see if she will tell me or if she wants to come over here herself and do it."

She dialed her mom and she answered right before voice mail. "What is it, honey?"

"That safe that you have in the bedroom, what's in it?"

"Legal papers, like our wills, papers on the house, some cash and rare coins. Why?"

"It looks like someone tried to break into it. Is there anyone that knows it's here besides me? Have you guys told anyone that you keep cash in the house or that you even have a safe? It's important for you to think and let me know. If there is something that important in here that they almost killed Brad for, then we should really take it out of here. If they decide to come back, the stuff will be gone, and hopefully they'll give up."

"I have the combination in my purse, let me get it for you. I just thought of something. I don't think that Brad knows the combination. Whenever we put anything in there, I always have to get my purse so we can open it. Oh my god, that's why he was beaten so badly, isn't it? He couldn't remember, so they tried to kill him, and when he still wouldn't give it to them, they shot him and left him for dead. This is awful, just awful. We're getting rid of that damn thing, there is nothing in there worth dying for, I assure you. Here it is, 24, 32, 78, 15. Now when you put it in, turn the handle all the way to the right, and it should open."

"Ok, I'll give it a shot. I'll let you know if I get it open or not, and if I do, I'll bring everything that's in it to you at the hospital."

"Ok, and, Sarah, as far as I'm concerned, you can blow the damn thing up."

Sarah smiled as she hung up and tried the combo that her mom gave her. The light changed to green, but they had done so much damage that the handle wouldn't turn.

"Oh, for crying out loud," she said and swore under her breath.

"What's the matter?" Layton asked.

"The assholes beat this up so bad that the handle won't turn so I can get the shit out of it."

"Let's see, can we just take it out of the floor? What did your mom say about anyone knowing it was here?"

"She said that no one knows about it as far as she knows and that Brad also didn't have the combo memorized, that she always had to get it out of her purse, she also said that if he couldn't remember it, that's probably why he got beaten up so badly, and when he still didn't tell them, they shot him and left him for dead."

"She might not be far off. I think it was more than one person. Brad's not a small guy, and there is no way one person could do all the damage in this house and to Brad. He wouldn't have let them either, especially knowing that your mom would be coming home anytime. So it could have played out like that, maybe they claimed to have a broken down car or something to get Brad to open the door. They beat him up a little bit, maybe tie him to the chair downstairs, and then they go searching the house for valuables. They find the safe and think they hit the jackpot. They go downstairs and ask Brad the combination, and he says he doesn't know. Gets beat up some more and threatened with a gun. He still doesn't know, so they shoot him and leave him for dead, come back upstairs and shoot at the safe in hopes it will open. It just pisses them off that much more that they can't get it open, so they try to force it open but no go. I'd say your mom might be right on about what happened. We won't know though, until Brad wakes up and tells us."

"I don't really see a way to get this out of the floor without destroying the floor. Can I go get Nate, he's pretty handy at breaking into things, maybe he'll know of a way to get this open."

"It's worth a shot, go get him."

Sarah ran down the stairs and outside to ask Nate to come in and see if he could figure out the safe.

"Just do me a favor and don't look around at anything, it's brutal in there, and if you aren't used to seeing stuff like that, you may not feel so great afterwards."

"Ok, I'll do whatever you want me to, I'm not really a big fan of blood."

"Good to know. Ok, c'mon, let's go back in there and see if we can figure it out."

She led him through the door, telling him to look to his left the whole way. They went up the stairs where there was no more gore, and she showed him the safe.

"Do you think you can open it, Nate?"

"Let me look at it."

She went through the rest of the upstairs and didn't notice anything else missing. She went back to her mom's room.

"What do you think? Can you get it open? I have the combination, but the handle won't turn because they messed the damn thing up."

"Let's see if we can pry it back and try it again."

After finding a screwdriver to use as a pry bar, they tried to move the handle so they could open it. It moved a little bit but not much. They needed something stronger.

"Let me run out to the garage, there must be something in there." Sarah turned to go, but Nate said, "Wait, let's try it now, it moved a little bit, maybe it was enough?"

She put the combination back in and they tried to open it again. With both of them pulling on it, the handle finally gave in and moved so they could open the door. When they looked inside, their mouths dropped open.

"I don't think I've ever seen that much cash in my entire life," Nate said in amazement.

"Neither have I. Mom said a little bit of cash and some rare coins. I see a lot of cash and nothing else. Maybe it is buried under all this money. Where did they get all this money? I need to grab her overnight bag and put her clothes in it, and then I need to grab another bag and put this stuff in it."

She pulled out the overnighter, threw some things in there for her mom, and found another duffel to put the stuff from the safe in.

When she was done, she asked the captain, "Is this considered evidence? They didn't get it, but it may be why they were here."

"I guess I would consider it more motive than evidence, but let's log it all before giving it to your mom, in case there are any questions since there are three of us as witnesses."

"Good idea."

34

All three of them counted the money and coins. They put the legal papers in the bottom of the bag, and the cash was placed on the top. There was $829,565 in the safe, and that was just the cash. Sarah and Nate went back to the hospital to give the bags to her mom. When they got there, she was sleeping in the chair next to Brad's bed.

Sarah went in and touched her hand and said, "Mom?"

"Huh? Oh, honey, have I been out long?"

"I don't know, we just got back. Can we talk in the hall please?"

Lynda followed Sarah into the hall where Nate was and asked, "What is it, honey?"

"We got the safe open finally. I thought you said there was only a little bit of cash in there."

"There is, along with some rare coins and legal papers."

"Mom, there was over $800,000. That's not just a little cash."

"Sweetie, calm down, it's under a million dollars, and you forget that I sell million-dollar homes, so that is just a little cash we keep it for emergencies."

"Can I be your next emergency? That's a lot of money. If you ever talked about it in front of anyone, that's probably why someone was there, they were going to rob you. Everything is in that other duffel, but I suggest you not leave it here."

"Can we bring it to your house? You have a safe, don't you?"

"No, I don't even have $800, what do I need a safe for? Besides, I like banks, they keep my money for me, and I don't worry about someone trying to kill me for it."

"We have money in the bank as well, this is really just for emergencies."

"I guess we'll have to bring it to my house. No one can know about this though. *No one.* The captain, Nate, you, and I are the only ones that know about it."

"Ok honey, whatever you say. When do you want to go to your place? I'm exhausted, and the nurses keep telling me that the doctor won't try to wake him up until tomorrow, and I really do need the rest."

"I'm ok with going now, how about you, Nate? Feel like bringing us home?"

"Anything I can do, I will."

They went in to say goodbye to Brad and that they'd be back in the morning.

When they were walking out to the car, Lynda asked, "What time does the dealership close where you wanted to get your new car from?"

"Eight o'clock I believe, why?"

"I'd like you to show me this car you want."

"Now? Can't it wait until tomorrow?"

"Oh, humor your old mother, will you please?"

"Ok, let's take her to see the car I want please, Nate."

"Sounds good to me. Wait until you see it, Lynda, it's a really beauty, just like your daughter."

"Then it must be off the charts."

They drove to the dealership, and the same salesman was there. She asked if they could take the car she drove yesterday out again for a ride and took Lynda for a ride.

She fell in love with it and said to Sarah, "You must buy this car, I love it! It's so sporty and fast."

"I was going to buy it today, but after what happened, I can wait."

"No, let's get it now."

"I don't feel like filling out all the paperwork today, how about if we come over tomorrow before we go to the hospital, and I can get it then?"

"No, we'll get it now." She reached into the duffel bag and pulled out a wad of money. She handed it to Sarah and said, "Count out what you need, consider it gift."

"This is one expensive gift, Mom."

"Nonsense, you only live once, and why not have the things you want? I have some money to share, and you need a car. Done and done. I feel better already. Brad's going to pull through, you just wait and see. He's going to live, and we are going to arrest those maniacs that tried to kill him. Over what, money and some coins?"

"Ok, let's go in and buy me a car. Look at that, I'm buying my first new car ever, or I should say, my mom is buying me my first new car ever. Thanks, Mom."

"You are more than welcome, my sweet child."

They went inside and bought Sarah her very first brand-new car. After that they stopped for some fast food, headed back to her house, stashed the duffel, said good night to Nate, and they got some much-needed sleep.

Sarah thought as she was drifting off to sleep, *Today wasn't the worst day ever, we might have figured out why Brad was attacked, and I got a new car but, I need to talk Mom and Brad into putting their money in the bank.*

35

When Lynda and Sarah got up the next morning, they headed to the hospital to check on Brad. He was still in the coma as nurse Stevens had told them he would be. His color looked a little bit better today, so that was a good sign. They took turns telling him about the new car Lynda had bought for Sarah and the rest of their day yesterday, just trying to do what the nurses suggested and treat him like normal. They had also brought his favorite book and were going to read to him when the doctor walked in.

"Good morning, Mrs. Hastings, how are you today? How does our patient look this morning?"

"I'm good, and he looks better than he did yesterday. Dr. Bower, this is my daughter, Sarah."

"Hello, Sarah, nice to meet you."

"Nice to meet you too, Dr. Bower."

"So, Dr. Bower, when do you think you will try to bring him out of the coma?" Lynda asked.

"I was thinking about later on today, I want to see how his vitals look in a little while, that will tell me if he is strong enough to bring him out of it."

"Oh, that is terrific news. Do you think there will be any issues with him waking up?"

"There shouldn't be. He hasn't been in it very long, and since he's showing signs of improvement, it should be fine."

"That's wonderful news."

"Mr. Hastings will probably be here for a while though, he was badly injured."

"I know it's going to be a long road, and I hope there are no lasting effects from the beating he took. I just can't believe that this happened. I appreciate everything that you're doing for him, Doctor."

"It is my pleasure, I'll be back after lunch to check on him and see if we are going to bring him out today."

"Thank you so much, we'll see you then."

Lynda looked at Sarah and said, "This is really good news. I can't wait for him to be out of that coma so we can try to find out what happened."

"He still might not wake up right away. He's on pain meds, and he has a lot of healing to do. Let's just see how he is after he is brought out of the coma. We can't push him, we don't want to slow down his healing in any way."

"You're right, of course, but I just want to see his eyes. If he is going to be ok, I'll be able to tell in his eyes."

"I'm going to go out and call Layton and let him know they might be bringing him out of the coma today. He might want to come over and see him. I honestly doubt if they will disconnect all of these machines today. They will probably leave them all there just in case something happens. I'll be back in a little bit, do you want me to go grab you anything from the cafeteria? You didn't eat breakfast, and you have to keep your strength up."

"You go talk to the captain. I'll be fine, but maybe a cup of coffee and a bagel or muffin would be good. Thanks, honey, I appreciate you looking out for me."

"Of course, Mom. You just read to Brad, and I'll be back."

Sarah went into the hall and called the captain to let him know that Brad might be taken out of the coma today. She was making her way to the cafeteria when her phone rang. It was Nate.

"Good morning, Nate," she answered.

"Good morning to you. How are you today? Enjoying driving your new car?"

"I'm doing well, and yes, I just love it."

"What's the news on Brad?"

"The doctor said that he might take him out of the coma today if his vitals show signs of improvement. His color is better today, so that's a win."

"Oh, that's great news, babe. Let me know if you need company, I'd be more than happy to come and sit with you and your mom if you need me to."

"Oh no, I totally forgot about our weekend until just now. Shit! I was really looking forward to it. I'm so sorry, Nate!"

"It's ok. I canceled everything after we got the news. We can do it some other time. You being there for your mom and Brad is way more important than us going away for the weekend."

"You are an incredibly sweet man. How did I get so lucky to meet you?"

"You had a crazy stalker, and I came to your rescue, so to speak."

"So to speak, I guess you did. Very glad it was you that the captain sent over."

"I feel like the lucky one. You're smart, ambitious, beautiful, and you are a fighter. I feel like I hit the jackpot when you said you'd go out with me."

"Aw, those are the nicest things anyone has ever said to me."

"Are you blushing? You always blush when I say nice things about you."

"I am." She laughed and said, "Thank you, Nate, for being there for me through my ordeal, and now this. I honestly don't know what I'd do if I didn't have someone else to talk to."

"I'll be here as long as you need and want me to be. Besides, I think I'm falling in love with you," he blurted out.

"What? Are you kidding me?"

"No, Sarah, I'm not. I can't seem to get you off of my mind. I'm always thinking about you, and I miss you when you aren't with me. I love spending time with you, and I think you are one of the best people I know. You've had to deal with some shit in your life, but it didn't break you, it made you stronger, and I really admire that about you. You take a challenge and meet it head-on, and you aren't afraid. You're really amazing to me." There was no response right away when he finished, so he said, "Sarah? Are you still there?"

"I'm here." She sniffled into the phone.

"What's wrong, why are you crying, did something happen to Brad?"

"No, it's nothing like that. I just can't believe all the nice things you just said to me. No one has ever said that many nice things about me. Except for my mom. You are a very special man, Nathan, and I feel like the lucky one. You've been so patient with me through all the business at my apartment, you make me feel safe, and you're just plain nice. You're handsome, kind, considerate, and I think I might be falling for you. I've told myself several times that I don't need anyone but myself, but when I'm alone, I find myself thinking about you and wishing that you were with me too. Look at us, a couple of saps," she said and giggled.

"I'll be your sap any day, Sarah Wheeler."

"And I will be yours too, Nathan Drake. I should really get back into Brad's room, but if you want to come over later, that would be ok with me, and I know my mom would like to see you again, she likes you too."

"Ok, you get back in with Brad, and I'll stop by later."

"Ok, see you later." She hung up the phone with a huge smile on her face and went to the cafeteria to get that coffee and a couple of muffins. When she walked back into Brad's room, he mom was reading to him and looked up. "Oh, thank you, dear. How's Nate?"

"How did you know that I called Nate?"

"Because you've been gone forever. Just kidding, sweetie, I can tell by the look on your face. He must have said something to you that you liked, you haven't stopped smiling since you came into the room."

"Oh, he did. We were supposed to go away this weekend, and I totally forgot, but he said it was no big deal, he took care of everything when we found out about Brad. Then he paid me some wonderful compliments and told me he thinks he's falling in love with me."

"Honey, that's wonderful, I'm so happy for you," she said, beaming.

"I told him I think I'm falling for him too. This time it's so much different and better. With Luke, I just couldn't get the suspicion out of my head that he had something to do with my kidnapping, but with Nate, he came in after the fact, so I knew he didn't have anything to do with my stalking. I told him if he wanted to stop down here later, we would be here." Just then the doctor came in and said, "Well, let's check his vitals to see if we take him out of this coma now or if we wait until tomorrow."

"I do hope it's today, Dr. Bower," said Lynda.

The doctor looked over Brad's chart and checked all the machines.

"I think we'll give it a try. His numbers have improved even since this morning, and that is very encouraging. He's definitely a fighter, Mrs. Hastings. Ok, I'm going to decrease his meds to help bring him out of the coma. He will probably be out until tomorrow, but you can certainly stay until visiting hours are over, and then I want you both to go home and get some rest. Once he is ready to wake up, he will. I'm also going to ask you to leave the room so that we can remove some of these tubes and machines. He won't look so scary after that's done. I'll go get a nurse and be right back to get that done."

"Thank you, Doctor, for everything. Thank you for explaining things to us, it helps a lot when you know what to expect. I think we'll go for a walk and give you some time to get him all situated." She leaned down and gave Brad a kiss on the cheek and told him they'd be back.

Sarah and Lynda left the room and went outside for some fresh air. "This is really great news," Lynda said excitedly.

"It really is, Mom, I'm so happy that he's improving, he's a strong man, and I'm sure he will heal quickly."

"I hope you're right. It's going to be a long road ahead of us for sure, but we'll do it together.

"I can come and help, too, if it gets to be too much on you, so don't be afraid to call on me."

"You're such a wonderful daughter. I know Brad thinks the world of you, so I'm sure he would be ok if you came over to take my place if I can't be there. I have to continue to work, but it's going to have to be on a limited basis for a little while at least. I'll have to talk to my boss about it soon too."

"I'm sure they will be fine with it. When I called about the showing you had, they were wonderful, and you're one of their top agents, I'm sure they won't have a problem with you taking time off. Besides, you have a ton of cash in case something happens."

"You're right, I'll just let him know that I'll finish up what I've got going right now but will have to turn down anything new until Brad is better."

They headed back into the hospital to see if they could go back in, and they were told they could. They went in to see that they had taken a lot of the things off of Brad, and he looked a lot better. He had a black-and-blue face, but not as many tubes sticking out of him.

"He looks better already," Lynda said with a smile on her face. "I suppose we can go home. If he's going to be sleeping until tomorrow, I'd like to get some sleep and something to eat, for some reason I'm starving."

"It's because you haven't eaten hardly anything in a couple of days, and I'll bet knowing that Brad will be waking up soon gives you some peace of mind."

"It really does. Let's go, honey. I'll just say goodbye."

She leaned over, whispered in his ear, kissed his cheek, and told him she loved him.

Sarah gave his hand a squeeze and told him she loved him too. They left the hospital knowing they would be spending countless hours here with him but optimistic that he was going to live.

About the Author

Mary lives in northern Minnesota and enjoys reading, gardening, cooking, fishing, crocheting, and writing. She enjoys time spent with family and friends and loves to snuggle and play with her dog. She enjoys new experiences with the ones she loves. She believes that no matter your age, never stop hoping and dreaming, because then you'll have nothing to aspire to. If you have nothing to aspire to, you stop living.